THE TIES THAT BIND

A MAX PLANK NOVEL

ROBERT BUCCHIANERI

Paula:

Thanks for saving this one when I was completely flummoxed.

ONE

Sarah Swan not only had the perfect name for a singer but also the looks and moves of a chanteuse.

And, more importantly, she could sing.

Her voice was fine, a smooth contralto, but she had that intangible quality that all the great ones have. At the upper ranges the notes had a little quaver, reminiscent of Judy Garland, which conveyed a deep sense of worldliness and pathos.

She sang mostly recent standards—Brel, Bacharach, the Beatles, and Sondheim, and gave each its full due, imbuing the generally downbeat lyrics with poignancy and a torchy charisma.

She was a tiny provocative thing with red hair, full lips, green eyes, and a lush figure.

The Black Canary had a ramshackle bluesy setting—a cabaret that had seen better times but clung to its dissolute charm: scuffed wood floors and tables, black and white photos of the jazz greats in action viewed through smoky prisms, a corner bar edged with strings of holiday lights, and dusty bronze candelabra illuminating the space from the black ceiling. Black canaries were sprinkled throughout the joint—little plastic and metal curios in back of the bar, paper cutouts hanging from the ceiling corners, and one large painting behind the stage, a small, round, elevated block of weathered hardwood in a jigsaw pattern.

Accompanying Ms. Swan on a spinet piano was a black man who looked to be in his late sixties and who performed without ever opening his eyes, his head swaying in time with his fingers. He hunched over the piano, which was easy for him to do, since he was, to possibly risk being politically incorrect, a hunchback. His playing was gorgeous, with surprising riffs and runs, lending vivid color to Ms. Swan's smoky vocals. A small drum set flanked the stage, and the drummer, a wafer-thin, completely bald woman wearing slacks and a man's white dress shirt and thin black tie, kept the music bouncing in time.

The room was full, maybe seventy people, all of whom seemed to be devotees of the singer. A good number of them leaned forward in their chairs, hanging on each elongated note or bated breath.

After she finished her set, I wandered to the bar, ordered a gin, and sidled up beside the stage next to the black curtain she and her band had disappeared behind.

A few minutes later, the curtain fluttered open, and the hunchback piano player wandered out. A cigarette was tucked between the index and middle fingers of his left hand. The fingers of his right hand were at his side, still riffing on imaginary keys. His rheumy, red-rimmed eyes skipped inquisitively around the room. He wore black leather pants, a powder blue shirt with a buttoned-up tweed vest, and a red beret tilted at a slight angle on his head.

Somehow it all worked. He was the most dapper-looking hunchback I'd ever seen.

His eyes eventually fell on me, and I nodded and raised my shot of Tanqueray to him with a little bow. He smiled, and I pointed to my glass and waved him over.

AFTER I BOUGHT HIM A BLANTON'S SINGLE BARREL KENTUCKY Whiskey and complimented on his playing, he commended me on my good taste in music and told me to call him Q. I was sorely tempted to ask him if that was short for Quasimodo, but somehow restrained myself. As opposed to the bell-ringer of Notre Dame, Q was quite distinguished looking and the hunch in his back much less pronounced.

We adjourned to a small table near the empty stage and continued chatting about jazz and the Black Canary and the San Francisco music scene in general, of which he was sharply critical.

It turned out that two of his favorite people were also mine: Beethoven and Fats Domino. So it took a little longer than I had planned to get to the reason I'd come out to the club on this cold, rainy, fog-infested night in the first place.

In the meantime, the female drummer appeared out of the back room. As she passed our table, she placed a caressing hand on his shoulder, leaned down, and kissed him on the cheek before she left.

"Phoebe, my girl," he whispered after her, watching her go. He turned to me and said, "Fine young lady that. And she's got chops. Too bad about everything else outside this club."

I raised my eyebrows and caught his eye, but he shook his head dismissively, indicating he wasn't going to tell me more. None of my damn business for sure.

But human curiosity being what it is, we, and by that, I mean me, are always fascinated by the intimate secrets of our fellow travelers on this crazy spinning little planet at the far, far reaches of the Milky Way.

Gossip is the heart and soul of human civilization.

If anybody asks, you can tell them that Max Plank told you that.

It was just after two a.m., and the band had completed their third and final set of the night.

That left Ms. Swan alone behind the black curtain.

"She's really good," I said.

"Phoebe or Sarah?"

"Both. But I'm talking about the singer."

He pursed his lips and nodded. "Sarah is more than damn good. She's one in a million. One of the best I ever worked with, and I worked with plenty, don't you know it."

"How long has she been at it?"

"Probably since she was a bouncing baby on her daddy's knee. She tells me that's all her folks ever told her was that they couldn't remember a time when she wasn't singing the whole day through." He paused, brought the orange-tipped paper tube full of bitter leaves to his lips and drew in a deep breath. He turned away from me and released a perfect ellipse into the air.

"They let you smoke?" I said. San Francisco has probably the strictest no smoking laws in the country, and the ban extends to all bars and nightclubs.

"Nope," he said, and continued, "Shame that girl don't have a record contract. Ten years ago, agents and A&R reps would have been throwing themselves at her feet, begging for a chance to make a record with her. Goddamn computers."

I wasn't sure exactly what he was getting at, but I understood him nonetheless.

"You been playing with her a long time?"

"'Since March sixteenth of last year."

"Pretty precise."

"Some days are so remarkable that you never forget them, even at my advanced state of decline."

"You don't look too bad, Q. In fact, you're jaunty as hell."

He chuckled, tapped the tip of his cigarette into a tiny plastic ashtray that he'd produced from inside his vest, coughed, and said, "Jaunty? I been called a lot a things in my life, but that's a first." He paused, scratching his nose with his forefinger while he seemed to be considering something. "What you here for, Max?"

"Good music."

"Yeah. Sure. But something else, too."

"You think so?"

"Yes, sir."

"You got me, Q."

He held my eyes and waited.

"I've been waiting for Ms. Swan to show herself."

"What business do you have with her?" For the first time, a defensive tone entered his voice.

"I'm afraid it's personal. I just need to ask her a few questions."

Q glanced at the bartender, a meaty middle-aged woman with bleached blond hair, a surprisingly large gold nose ring, and a no-nonsense manner. A look passed between them that carried a hint of a tribal secret. Outsiders beware.

"We're like a family here. You seem like a nice guy, a respectable sort. But I have to tell you that Felix and Stanley over there," he pointed to the front of the club, a table tucked into a dark corner where two beefy bruiser-types were playing cards, "don't take kindly to anyone annoying Sarah."

"Last thing I want to do is irritate anyone here."

"What is it that you want with her?"

I considered my options. Sarah was likely to emerge from the back room any moment now, and it was a free country if I wanted to talk with her. Or I could take my leave and then follow her home and talk to her there, although a stranger approaching in the middle of the night might probably spook her.

"I don't understand why you're worrying so much about me and what I might ask Ms. Swan, Q. But I can already see what kind of man you are, and I respect that. I do need to ask her some questions. Would it make you feel better if you sat in on our little chat?"

He shot me a piercing gaze that could have pinned me to the wall like a dead insect had it the force of motion. Finally, he said, "All right. I think you're being straight with me. You've been trying to play me, but if I was to guess, you don't mean no harm. If she wants to talk to you, we'll do it out here in front of God and me and Felix and Stanley, but none of us need listen in. If she don't want to talk to you, then I'm politely going to ask you to leave. Understood?"

"Sounds fair."

"I'll go ask her if she wants to meet you." He squashed the cigarette out in the tiny ashtray, gripped the table with both hands, and prepared to rise.

A loud cracking boom exploded from the back of the club, followed by a woman's scream. Something heavy, metallic, clattered to the floor, and right after, something else made a gut-wrenching thudding sound. Q fell back into his chair at the same time I jumped to my feet. As the echo of the sounds reverberated throughout the room, I hurried toward the black curtain, vaguely aware of the two bulky bodies racing right behind me.

I threw back the curtain on a small room, part dressing area complete with vanity and oval mirror with lots of small photos clipped to its edges, and part storage room. Boxes of wine and liquor were stacked against the walls. The floor was painted black, the ceiling decorated with moon and star stickers lending a dusky glow to the space.

A door at the back of the room drifted open. It led to a back alley that ran behind the club.

Sarah Swan lay crumpled in the middle of the room beside a chair spilt over on its side. She was moaning softly, clutching her stomach with both hands, blood gushing over her trembling fingers.

At that moment, Felix and Stanley, followed by Q, pushed me out of the way and knelt beside the wounded singer.

I raced out the back door and into the dark alleyway.

TWO

The first thing I noticed outside was how quiet it was after the chaotic panic of the room I'd just left.

There were three large dumpsters in front of me, each spilling over with garbage. A mangy black and white cat with shocked yellow eyes sat on top of one of them, his glowing eyes fixed on me, ready to pounce away.

The presence of the cat convinced me that the slim chance that whoever shot the singer was still nearby, perhaps hiding behind a dumpster, was nil.

The street beneath my feet was rough and wet, and the night air was cold, the fog thick. I paused, closed my eyes, and listened.

After just a few seconds, a sound came to me from the distance.

I squinted and tried to see through the gloom. About thirty yards away, a pair of running shoes below dark-colored jeans dangled, rising up in the air until they disappeared in the drifting fog.

I galloped forward, quickly reaching a wall made of weathered gray brick roughly seven feet high. I heard someone drop down on the other side and steps scampering away.

I searched the uneven surface for the way up and spotted gaps in the brick. I reached up and hooked my fingers around the lowest and closest rough slash and vaulted up. In seconds, I stood on top of the wall, a bleeding cut on the edge of my forefinger, a product of my haste. I spotted a fleeing figure wearing a hoodie rounding a corner maybe fifty feet ahead of me.

The alleyway was flanked by the backs of stores and industrial supply houses off Third Street and Arthur Avenue, not too far from San Francisco's India Basin docks.

The shooter had turned on a corner lit dimly by a street lamp. The fog continued to drift close to the ground, bending and shaping the night with otherworldly shadows.

I turned and found purchase for my feet, scrambling down two steps before leaping clear of the wall. I raced around the corner and pulled up short, assessing my surroundings, searching for the hoodie.

I found myself in a concrete rhomboid roughly the size of a playground basketball court. An engineering firm's offices lay directly in front of me, a property management outfit on my left. Ahead of me there was another narrow alleyway that, if it didn't dead end, might spill out of this otherwise walled in space.

I stayed still and listened and, after just a few seconds, detected the sound of fumbling at a doorknob, the clink and ratchet of a key somewhere in the darkness to the left of me.

I trotted toward the noise, veering close to the concrete wall on my left--the sound of a door closing just before I reached Marco Polo Designs and then the Children's Rescue Network and a sign for the Bacchus Management Group.

Light filtered under the door of the Children's Network, the only evidence of life in the whole triangle. I stood in front of the metal-framed door attempting to commune telepathically, trying to force it to give up its deep, dark secrets. After that didn't work, I knocked on the wood surface and waited. I noticed a little tarnished gold bell encased in a copper trimming to the right of the door and pressed on it for a few seconds.

I was just about to test the strength of the door with my shoulder when I heard movement inside, and then a gap opened wide enough to pull taut a thick chain anchored to the opposite wall.

A stout woman in her thirties wearing a San Francisco Giants sweatshirt with a hood and a black baseball cap turned backward looked at me with an unfriendly expression on her face.

The hoodie was red, not black. She wore purple Crocs, not black running shoes. Detective work is never that straightforward or easy, dammit.

"Evening," I said.

She frowned. "Can I help you?"

"There's been a shooting," I crooked a thumb and pointed it back, "at the Black Canary. I followed someone running away, and I think they may have ended up here."

She narrowed her eyes.

"Has anyone entered here in the past few minutes?"

"No," she said curtly.

"I thought I heard a door opening, this door right here, as a matter-of-fact." I tapped on it with the knuckles on my left hand, driving my point home.

She didn't seem to like that. She pulled away, as if I were about to strike her.

Wrong move, Plank. Sometimes I act a bit rashly, but jeez, an attempted murderer was on the loose, no?

She stood with her hands on her hips and assessed me through the slim opening. "No one has come in here...Mr...."

"Plank. Max. And I'm speaking with?"

"Liz. Listen, I haven't heard a thing. Whoever you're after isn't here."

"I need to take a look inside," I said.

"I'm afraid I'll have to say no. There are children here. They've been abandoned or abused. The risk to them is too great. Maybe you're telling the truth, maybe not. Either way, I can't let you in."

"Police are on the way. They'll be here soon."

She folded her arms high on her chest, climbing up on her high horse. "Fine. I'll talk to them then."

"All right. Thanks for your time," I mumbled, then turned and kicked the door hard. The chain broke, the door flew open, and I stepped inside and right up in charming girl's shocked face.

"Sorry, Liz. But there's a murderer on the loose, and I think he or she is hiding in here."

"You can't do this!" she cried and put her hands on my chest.

I shrugged her off, stepped around, and moved forward past a tiny reception area with a nice, new walnut-hued desk fronting two comfy leather chairs. There were photos of happy children playing in parks on the walls and various contact posters for social service agencies, including Contact and San Francisco Sex Information, a suicide prevention line and sexual counseling line, respectively.

I followed a dark hallway back into the interior of the building with Liz shouting for me to stop and calling out the name Scott repeatedly.

By the time I got to a large open area that was a combination of a playroom and children's library, a man rolled into the room from an adjacent area.

Yes, I said "rolled." He was in a wheelchair.

"Scott?" I said.

"What are you doing here?" he said, his hands rising, his fists clenched. Scott was older, likely in his fifties, and looked to be quite tall. He had a lean, wiry look to his face and upper body, but had a modest paunch resting on his lap. His chin and gaze projected firmness and strength.

He wore a gray pullover sweater, dark blue jeans, and thick black socks without shoes.

I held up my hands, palms outward. "There's been a shooting, and I followed the suspect here. I heard the outside door open, and he disappeared inside."

Scott looked over my shoulder at Liz.

"I've been out front the whole time. I didn't let anyone in."

"I think the suspect had keys to the place," I said.

"No way. Nobody came through that door. Nobody ever does this time of night, except for a child every once in a great while. I've been here for three hours and never left the front office." Liz was determined to remain uncooperative. Maybe she was right, considering the vulnerabilities of her charges.

She did sound convinced and convincing, but I was having none of it. "Lookit, I heard someone enter. I mean no harm to anyone here, but the singer at the Black Canary has been wounded, and I need to search this place to make sure the shooter isn't hiding here."

"Where are the police?" Scott asked, the grip in his hands loosening. He laid them back down on the rubber wheelchair armrests.

"On the way. But every moment counts. By the time they get here, the suspect might be long gone. Please, help me."

Scott again glanced at Liz, then nodded. His gaze returned to me and he said, "I'm the Executive Director here. We do this my way. Right?"

I nodded, and he spun the wheelchair with the skill of a NASCAR driver. I followed him farther back into the building.

THERE WASN'T ALL THAT MUCH TO SEARCH. THERE WERE A TOTAL OF

three other small offices, and we quickly determined no place to hide in any of them. I checked a couple of closets, feeling foolish. I didn't find any black hoodies hanging from swaying coat hangers.

The only remaining rooms to check were the children's dormitories. There were two—one for girls, the other for boys.

Liz was dead set against letting me into either of them, telling me the children were sound asleep, had suffered enough trauma in their lives, and a big, strange man at night might induce even more nightmares.

I know how damn scary I am, but I convinced Scott that I'd be quiet as a church mouse and tiptoe my way quickly through the tulips. My argument that it would be irresponsible to risk a murderer possibly lurking in the children's bedrooms seemed to make some kind of sense to him.

There was room for as many as twenty children stacked in bunkbeds in each room. The boys room currently held seven, and the girls nine. Once again, the search didn't take long. There weren't many hiding places. The spaces under the bunkbeds were too tight for even a rat, let alone a human being. I gave each berth a quick once over. All the children, save one little girl of about eight, were fast asleep. The little girl, startled awake as I walked by, sat up in bed staring at me with wide terrified eyes. Scott immediately went to her, whispered in her ear while petting her shoulder, and in a few seconds, she laid back down and closed her eyes.

As I exited the children's rooms, which lined the back wall of the building, I noticed a small kitchen area featuring a small, round granite table with two more fine leather chairs, a spanking new microwave, a fancy, gold-plated espresso machine like the kind you see behind coffee bars in Rome, a water cooler, and a wall full of built-in teak cabinets.

The place didn't seem to be your typical non-profit social service agency, struggling to get by with minimal funding. Some of the accoutrements here rivaled what you'd find at a fancy downtown law firm.

I noticed a sturdy back door with a deadbolt lock.

"Where does that go?" I pointed at the door.

"Out to an alley. It's where we put our garbage for pickup. Leads back out to the street."

"Can I have a look?"

He looked up at me from his wheelchair perch and shrugged.

I didn't wait for a full approval. I moved to the door, slid open the deadbolt and stepped out into a narrow alleyway framed by a high wooden fence. Two dumpsters and one large rubber garbage can sat to the right of the entrance. To the left, the dusky street led to a roughly six-foot-high concrete barrier with another door that was currently propped open. I trotted the fifty or so feet to the door and had a looksee. It opened out onto the greater world.

If the shooter escaped through the Children's Network offices, as I was sure he did, he probably disappeared here. Someone had locked the deadbolt behind him.

I returned to the offices, thanked Scott, and nodded to Liz, who gave me a disgusted look, and took my leave.

I SEARCHED THE REST OF THE TRIANGLE, JOGGING PAST A HALF-dozen trucks and semis and a eighteen wheeler, to the end of the alley letting out to Quint Street. There was another wall fencing in the area, and it was pretty high, but scalable by any desperado running for his life, so the shooter could have escaped that way too.

But I didn't think so.

AS I JUMPED BACK DOWN FROM THE WALL ONTO THE ALLEY

fronting the Black Canary, I found myself facing two members of San Francisco's finest pointing Sig Sauer revolvers at me.

I put my hands up high and let them spin-tumble-dry-me until they were satisfied I wasn't armed. I told them who I was as enigmatically as I could get away with, and gave them the short version of my story, finishing with the fact that Q, among others at the club, could vouch for me. When I mentioned the Children's Network and my investigation there, they both frowned on cue.

Most cops don't much like guys like me. They consider what I do to be amateur hour or vigilante interference.

I've found that you can't please all the people all the time.

A life lesson you can take to the bank and deposit, and it'll pay you compound interest.

They escorted me back to the club none too politely.

BY THE TIME WE GOT BACK TO THE BLACK CANARY, AN AMBULANCE had taken Sarah away, and cops had blanketed the club like a plague of cranky locusts.

One officer kept me cornered while the other huddled with Q and the bartender. Q looked up from the officer a couple of times and glanced in my direction, but his expression stayed expressionless.

After a few minutes, the officer talking to Q turned and nodded at the cop guarding me, who then muttered, "Okay. Detective Marley will need to speak with you." He dragged a chair over and said, "Sit down there and don't move till I come get you."

"Do you have any idea how the singer is doing?" I asked.

"Do I look like a doctor?"

"Now that you mention it..."

"Just sit down and shut up."

"Yes, sir," I barked, mimicking a buck private's response to a surly drill sergeant.

He had his back turned to me, and my tone of voice stopped him in his tracks. He pivoted, shot me a look, and said, "You being a smart ass, asshole?"

"If I were you, I wouldn't use ass and asshole in the same sentence, at least not so close together. I don't know that it's grammatically incorrect, but it just doesn't hit the ear in a pleasing manner."

"Fuck you." He looked like he'd like to smack me one. I do have a knack for bringing out the best in people.

"Sticks and stones," I murmured.

"Fuck you," repeated, hammering his point home before leaving me all alone.

DETECTIVE MARLEY AND I SAT AT THE TABLE IN THE FRONT OF THE club that Felix and Stanley had used for their card game.

He was a small man in every sense of the word. He couldn't have been over five foot three and had a small head, tiny ears, a snippet of a nose, and smaller than average eyes in his small face. The biggest thing about him was the chip on his shoulder.

"I don't understand why you chased after the suspect. You didn't even know the girl. You didn't know anybody here. You just a hero at heart or some kind of vigilante wannabe?"

"Hmmm," I said, touching my finger to my lips and looking up at the ceiling reflectively. "Let me think...hero at heart or vigilante wannabe? Tough choice. Can I get back to you later?"

Marley shook his head as if he couldn't believe a jerk off like me was sitting in front of him. So, he doubled down on sassiness. "Couldn't get a date or do you go out all by your lonesome often to hear music?"

"Jeez, Detective, you're a master at confusing me with your dual choice conundrums."

"Lookit, asshole, a woman has been shot. She may not make it.

You want to keep on joking around, maybe we can take you down to the precinct and let you entertain the other inmates with your jokes."

"You're sending little shivers up and down my spine, Detective."

"What the hell were you doing here tonight, and why did you chase down a suspect?"

Despite my inclinations, I decided to try to be reasonable. "I'm doing some investigative work for a client, which involves a couple of people at the club."

"You're a P.I.?"

"No."

"What are you then?"

Not the first time somebody's asked me that. "It's complicated. I help people out sometimes. Strictly personal."

"That's peachy, Plank. So, what's this investigation all about?"

"Sorry. Not at liberty to discuss it. I'm not trying to be difficult, but I can't get into it without my client's approval."

"You're treading awfully close to the line here. Maybe hauling you in front of a judge for impeding a police investigation would help you see things right."

"C'mon, Detective. This isn't about me and my asking a few questions. Have you sent officers to that Children's Network? I'm telling you the suspect disappeared there."

"You telling me how to do my job?"

I sighed. "Wouldn't think of it. Just telling you what I know. You're talking to all the others here. They know as much as I do. We all heard the shot and reacted. I don't know anything more about it. I chased the suspect but didn't catch him. Didn't see his face. I told you what he was wearing. Don't have a clue as to his or her motivation. As you said, I don't know the singer or anyone else here."

It went back and forth like this for a while before Marley

decided he'd had enough. He told me to stay right where I was until they finished talking to all the witnesses.

AFTER ALMOST AN HOUR, Q SHOWED UP AT MY LONELY TABLE. HE sat down with a weary sigh. His eyes studied the table; his fingers gripped the edges.

"You okay?"

"Fuckin' life," he muttered under his breath.

I put my hand on his arm. "Have you heard anything about Sarah?"

"They haven't told me a damn thing. Probably don't know. They won't let me go yet."

"What hospital did they take her to?"

"San Francisco General is what the ambulance guys told me." For the first time, he looked up and into my eyes. He looked like he'd aged ten years in the past hour. He closed his eyes.

"Any idea who might have done this?"

He opened his eyes. "Everybody loves Sarah. She ain't got an enemy in this godforsaken world."

"You haven't noticed anything unusual lately? Anything different about how she's been acting? Anybody hanging around here that, thinking about it now, didn't seem right, didn't seem like they belonged?"

"Police just asked me the same kinds of things. I don't know. I don't think so. I got to get out of here and go see about Sarah."

"Okay."

"You got a phone on you?"

I reached in my coat and handed him my cell phone.

"Hate these things," he said, looking at it as if it might bite him. "How the hell you dial it?"

"Here, let me do it."

He placed the phone back in my palm and gave me a number. I punched it in and handed the phone back to him.

He brought it to his ear, and a moment later, I heard a woman's voice. Q said, "Phoebe, honey, sit down, won't you. Go ahead. Okay. Okay. I need you to get on over to the General Hospital...what...I don't know...it's Sarah, honey, she's been shot...shit...yes..."

While I listened, my heart pounding, my adrenaline spiking again, I thought back to forty-eight hours before and what had brought me here tonight in the first place to question a woman who, by the lights of her friends here, was a much different person from the evil femme fatale my client had described.

THREE

That crisp, cool, September morning, Alexandra woke me up with a call as she was getting on a plane to London. She reminded me that I was responsible for picking up Frankie at school and, by the way, she was already missing me.

I told her I missed her, too. Which was a little white lie.

At that very moment I didn't miss her, but knew I would soon enough.

Through my porthole, I could see that it was shaping up to be a lovely day with a clear blue sky.

I was ensconced in the cabin of my houseboat, *Acapella Blues*, a fully-reimagined World War II lifeboat, docked at the end of a rotting gangway on Pier 39, Fisherman's Wharf, San Francisco, when, for some reason, some old lyrics started playing through my mind.

Some days are diamonds.

Some days are stones.

I tried to recall the song they came from.

It took me a few seconds to remember the singer, John Denver.

I'd been dragged to one of his concerts by a golden-haired female I was hankering after. Her devotion to the still boyish troubadour almost put me off her, but she was an otherwise exuberant woman, an entomologist fascinated by parasitic wasps. Come to think of it, that alone should have warned me away. But in the several months of our sporadic affair, she enlightened me to the point of a strange affection for the benefits of a species that laid their eggs in the bodies of unwitting hosts.

Besides, I couldn't resist her name, Veronica, or her long, lithe form.

To my surprise, I thoroughly enjoyed the show and felt a pang of loss at the singer's demise, as this was only a few months before Denver died crashing his experimental glider into the Pacific Ocean.

Far Out.

But Denver didn't write the song, which was penned by a country singer named Dick Feller, who, later in life, admitted to being a transgendered human now living as a woman.

Some days are diamonds.

Some days are stones.

My unexpected visitor put a damper on my immediate plans, but I had to admit that her case was not altogether unwelcome, although I wished I could turn her offer down.

The woman facing me at the breakfast table reminded me of my aunt Florence. She had stiff-slick silver hair, high cheekbones in the early stages of collapse, a very large irregularly-shaped nose, and triangular diamond-studded earrings swaying back and forth from her tiny ears as she gesticulated, explaining her problem.

She was dressed beautifully with an air of preciseness about her, but, for the sake of accuracy if not generosity, she was not a beauty. Those cheekbones, which often form the base of classic beauty, in her case clashed with otherwise blunt facial features. Big nose, small eyes, pinched brow, and thin, judgmental lips.

I hadn't much liked Aunt Florence, who was a beautiful woman but always seemed to subtly convey the notion that her family was wealthier and more accomplished than my own. The fact that it was true only served to aggravate more. But I wasn't going to judge my new potential client negatively for her unwitting resemblance to my hardly dear, now departed aunt.

As I listened to Mrs. Wambaugh with one ear, I kept the other alert for any sign of dinner, the tell-tale *click* of the fishing rod shoved in a tube off the stern of the boat. My eyes took in her dangling earrings.

Earrings have always fascinated me. Whoever thought of decorating ears?

"So, do you think you might be willing to look into this for me, Mr. *Plank?*"

I pursed my lips, mimicking a mind in deliberation. "Perhaps, Mrs. Wambaugh."

"Money is not a consideration."

People like Mrs. Wambaugh had obviously transcended the needs and wants of the average mundane life. Most people, even in prosperous but declining America, were stuck on the lowest level of Maslow's Hierarchy of Needs, enmeshed in the struggle to breathe, feed, have sex, and excrete. If Mrs. Wambaugh had ever had any trouble with any of those, I was sure that they were minor skirmishes, quickly dispatched, before effortlessly moving on to higher ground.

She'd most likely been born to money, or married it. She didn't look the entrepreneurial type to me.

Nevertheless, I'd been idle for too long. I'd been turning down offers for many months, ever since my encounters with the unsavory characters in Frankie's case.

Perhaps because Frankie lived with Alexandra now, and I was, more or less, a surrogate dad, I still thought of the case often. I couldn't seem to get the bad taste out of my mouth.

Maybe I should have taken something else right away as it was unlikely I would meet a similar cast of ne'er-do-wells. Alas, my nature tends toward avoidance rather than confrontation. At least until I'm fully engaged.

But now I was a little on edge. For too long I'd been out of the fray, floating along on calm waters. I was getting a bit rough around the edges, loose in the cage, accustomed to ease.

Marsh and Bo were getting a little impatient with me.

I looked out the port window of *Acapella Blues* and studied the Cadillac limousine my guest had arrived in. Silver, shiny, sleek, just like her, although its cheekbones were new and free of wear and tear. A tall, curly-haired, muscular man of about thirty, dressed in a dark suit, leaned against the driver's side door, listening to his iPod, his eyes hidden beneath teardrop shades.

The case was not exactly in my wheelhouse. I normally tried to stay out of the sticky wicket of family affairs—adultery, incestual relations, parental meddling in its various disguises. Although, upon reflection, I'm aware that just about any case ends up entangled somehow with family.

"How did you find me?"

"My lawyer referred me to you." Her eyes bounced around the cabin of the boat, her eyebrows raised, her nose rising, as if she'd just sniffed a rotting rat carcass.

My boat has that effect on people. Mia casa, be it ever so humble.

I don't normally like to meet clients here, but somehow she'd found me and showed up unexpectedly right before breakfast. Rude, but one of the perils of living on a boat. Since it didn't have a solid foundation or front door, people often don't respect it like a traditional home.

"What's his name?" I asked.

"My lawyer?"

"He of whom we are speaking."

"Mr. Raditch. Of Reed, Raditch, Spengler, Feedle, and Fitzhugh."

Of course. RRRSF&F.

I'd heard the name, but thankfully had never encountered any of the raconteurs represented by the bold letters in real life.

"Offices in the financial district?" A firm with that many names could only be located close to money.

She shook her head dismissively. "Atherton."

One of the most expensive zip codes in the country. The tiny peninsula hamlet was the most conservative town in the Bay Area.

"And you?"

"We have local residences on Nob Hill and in Atherton."

I was sure that non-local residences abounded. "And what nice things did Mr. Raditch have to say about me?"

"To be honest, it wasn't all that nice. He expressed reservations, along with grudging admiration." She paused, nodded, obviously agreeing after meeting the subject in question.

I was willing to take acclamation any way I could get it.

Her eyes narrowed and quickly frisked me again, from head to toe. Despite the fact that I was my usual stylish self—a tattered seersucker shirt, with only a couple of stains, unbuttoned to mid-chest, dirty khakis, and bare feet—she seemed unimpressed, if not downright put off. If she hadn't arrived so unexpectedly, I might have at least buttoned my shirt. I wondered if she'd tried to call me. I'd have to check my cell phone. At times, I have a tendency to forget that I possess one, but lately, Alexandra and Frankie have been forcing me to keep it close on a more frequent basis.

"...but, he said that you had a reputation in certain quarters for...a kind of...gritty effectiveness."

"I see." I try not to let such high praise go to my head.

"He mentioned that you were willing to...perhaps take on cases of a less savory character with the proper sense of discretion."

That was me all over. You could always count on Max Plank to keep your nasty secrets.

"Needless to say, decorum is essential in my situation."

"So, to summarize, you believe that your son is involved with a woman who is taking advantage of him? That she is hiding something and may be interested in his money, his name, and little else."

"Yes. But it's more than that really. I believe he may be in some danger. I want you to investigate her fully. There must be something in her past...she's a gold digger if I've ever met one. And, even more importantly, she has the stink of evil about her. It's palpable. She's dangerous to Christopher and to all of us in the family."

"What makes you think so?"

She sighed and closed her eyes. When she opened them, her face had taken on that frightening look of steel-eyed determination that can only be mustered by women of a certain age and social status.

"I'd say it's just woman's intuition, but believe me, there's more. Sarah is admittedly attractive in a way that some men find hard to resist, but there's a wealth of experience etched on her face and in her eyes. She's seven years Mikey's senior, he's only twenty-four, and knows how to play him. To fiddle with him."

She shook her head dismissively.

"Some men don't mind being fiddled with." Not to name names.

She gave me a look. "I am quite aware of what lurks in the minds of men." She sniffed, tweaked her nose with her pinky, and continued, "And Mikey is under her spell. Still, he's my son. I love him. I'm afraid for him."

I had the ungenerous feeling that perhaps she was more afraid of losing some of the family fortune and reputation than any great feeling for her child.

"Do you have other children?"

"A daughter."

"And?"

"She has nothing to do with this."

So, two problem children then. After chatting with Mrs. Wambaugh for just a few minutes, this wasn't a big surprise.

"You still haven't told me anything specific. In what way has she taken advantage of your son?"

"In the same ways that women have been taking advantage since time immemorial."

Oh. Of course. So obvious. "I understand how you feel. But can you give me just a bit more detail to help—"

An unmistakable shadow fell across the open door to the boat.

Mrs. Wambaugh looked up, startled by the figure in the doorway.

Marsh Chapin generally has that effect on people.

He bowed, lowered his hand with an elegant twirl toward the rich lady, who stared at it as if it might bite, and said, "Madame, Marsh, at your service. I would recommend that you leave this sorry excuse for a dwelling and join me for a drink onshore where I will regale you with horror stories about our friend here that will freeze your heart mid-pulse. I don't know how Maxwell coaxed you here, but I daresay there was little in the way of truth involved."

"Mrs. Wambaugh, this is Marsh Chapin, a recent escapee from the lockdown ward of a facility it's best not to mention in polite company," I quipped deadpan.

She stared at Marsh, then turned her back to him with a distinct look of displeasure, obviously not used to such witty repartee.

"I can certainly understand why Jeffrey had reservations about you, Mr. Plank," she huffed.

"Jeffrey?"

"Mr. Raditch."

"Yes, well, my associate, Mr. Chapin, does sometimes have a tendency to violate rules of order. But he means well, mostly."

"May we continue?" she said, sounding like she might be getting ready to rap one's fingers with a ruler.

"What?" Marsh raised his eyebrows, opened his palms.

I motioned with my chin. Marsh walked through the cabin and disappeared behind the door to the back of the boat. Sometimes Marsh can't help himself and forgets that I have a professional reputation to protect.

Sort of.

I turned back to my prospective client. "What does Sarah Swan do for a living?"

"She's a singer, I gather. Mikey is entranced with her talent."

"Have you heard her sing?"

She frowned, as if the notion was preposterous and I was an idiot for asking. She did not deign to answer.

"Does she perform professionally?"

"Mikey tells me she performs several shows every weekend at an establishment called the Black Canary in the city," she said, then snapped, "now will you or won't you take the case?"

"One little matter I need clarified before I give you my decision."

She had me at "money is no consideration," but cash, although I was running a little short due to my inherent tendency to drift along in life and the recent additional expenses revolving around Frankie, is almost never my primary motivation.

"Once I start, I have a slight bulldog tendency. I normally follow my cases through to the end, no matter where they lead. Should you find yourself dissatisfied with the information I uncover, that is certainly your prerogative, but your prerogative may have little bearing on my efforts. Therefore, I insist upon a significant retainer, all of which will be accounted for meticulously by my accountant, Ms. Smith, with any unused funds refunded in full."

Mrs. Wambaugh held my gaze for a long time before answering. "Fine." She opened a small black felt purse tucked at her side and extracted a small white envelope. She extended her hand to me, and I took it and flipped the flap open to find five stacks of hundred-dollar bills bound with neat strips of white ribbon.

"Will that do," she said, and it wasn't a question. She was used to getting what she wanted, and the envelope had left nothing to chance.

I glanced at her ears, the diamonds glistening, and nodded. "That will," I said, rubbing my thumb over the greenbacks.

FOUR

"Ms. Smith, the accountant? I'm surprised I've never met the lady," Marsh said as soon as I joined him at the back of the boat.

"You know how it is with number crunchers. They stay holed away in their cubicles in front of their adding machines."

"Adding machines?"

"Whatever."

"Don't you think a woman like her already knows a whole heck of a lot about you before she engages?"

I shrugged. "Do you know her?"

"Of her," Marsh said. "The Wambaughs are very old money, at least in California years. Her great grandfather built his fortune peddling a series of miracle elixirs with a traveling medicine show he started, Wambaugh's Wizard Oil Company, during the California Gold Rush in the mid-nineteenth century. I guess it was a pretty entertaining carnival type thing with magicians, a freak show, a flea circus, comics, and storytellers."

Marsh paused, rose from his sling-back canvas chair, walked to the edge of the boat, and took a long sip of black coffee while staring out toward the Bay and Treasure Island, before continuing. "But the main purpose was always to sell the magic elixir. It promised to cure every malady known to man, from heart disease to arthritis to cancer, extending your life, along with smoothing out your facial wrinkles and removing the stains from your clothes. It was all snake oil, of course, but you usually got at least a hit of cocaine, alcohol, or opium for your trouble and your money. He was smart enough to get out of the business before some intrepid newsman started exposing it all for the scam it was. He started buying real estate, and that's what still pays the bills and then some. His son, Douglas, your client's father, really expanded the business, building an empire, making it one of the top five developers in the country. Apartment buildings, shopping centers. In the eighties, they went into Vegas and own quite a number of apartment buildings there now and at least one casino that I'm aware of."

I noticed a tugging at the end of my fishing pole and leaped to grab it. I waited a few seconds, then yanked it and felt...nothing. I reeled in, put another piece of bait on the line, and cast it out about fifty yards from the boat.

I sat back down across from Marsh.

"So, what's the problem?" he said.

"A son. A gold digger. Fear of fleecing and—"

"Blackmail, hearts broken, trusts sundered, estates ransacked..."

"You've got the idea. By the way, what about the husband? Mrs. Wambaugh mentioned she was married but nothing more as to his involvement in all this."

"He's a bit of a mystery from what I've read. I guess he's estranged from the family. He had a reputation as a kind of hanger-on, a gigolo of a sort, before he married Mrs. Wambaugh. She didn't take his name, kept daddy's, the company's—Fogerty is his name. He kind of disappeared years ago."

"Maybe see if you can find out a little more about him."

"Okay. Anything else?

"Not at the moment. I'm not sure there's really anything here but a meddling mother's paranoia and jealousy. I'll do an initial quick surveillance to check on the girl. Have a chat with people at the nightclub where she works and check out the places she hangs, etcetera, etcetera."

Marsh nodded.

I'm a big guy, and so is Marsh, but there's something about him, an aura that comes off him, that quickens the pulse of any room he walks into. He's a handsome devil with golden hair and quick steel-colored eyes. He doesn't have bulging, weight-lifter muscles, but he's cut and lithe as a panther and just as dangerous.

"You didn't come out here to discuss the Wambaughs with me."

He winced, scratched his head, looked away. "Dao."

I waited while my pulse quickened.

"I was visiting him on the *Sweet and Sour* last night discussing the plans for the Kabuki theater and...I don't know. It's nothing I can put my finger on specifically, but he's not his usual chipper self. He's really preoccupied. Very unlike him. He wasn't really involved when I started talking about the theater, and you know how passionate he is about that project. He's trying his best not to let it show. That typical Zen calm exterior has a crack in it."

"Did you ask him about it?"

"Yes. But he just brushed me off."

"So maybe it's just a spat with Meiying or an investment that's underperforming, even Dao has to have one of those every once in a great while."

"I don't think it's that simple."

"Still, maybe he was just having a bad day."

He frowned. Marsh isn't one to jump to conclusions. He has a very logical mind and tries to eliminate emotions from any calculus unless whatever he's measuring is affected by them. He prides himself on his lack of personal feeling in most matters. But he does seem to have a sixth sense about trouble. His gut instincts are rarely wrong. His atavistic, reptilian brain is developed far beyond that of most mere mortals.

"I think it's something serious. And he won't tell me because he's afraid of what I might do."

I nodded. Dao was aware of Marsh's preferred way of handling problems and didn't really approve. He abhorred violence, but on at least one occasion, Marsh's method had been necessary and Dao thankful for it.

"Okay. We've got a cribbage game scheduled in a couple of days. I'll see how he's doing and talk to him if I pick up on the same vibe."

"Lunch is calling," Marsh said.

I followed his eyes to my quivering pole and leapt to my feet.

FIVE

After Detective Marley let us go around four a.m., I drove Q to the hospital and waited with him and Phoebe until we could get a doctor to talk to us.

He was a big, round guy settled deeply into his forties, with plump cheeks and sad eyes. He wore an ID badge with a grainy, unflattering photo. His white smock had a splatter of blood drops near one pocket.

"I'm Dr. Newburgh," he said, and brought his cupped hands up to his face, rubbed his nose with his forefingers, then tucked them beneath his armpits. "She's still being operated on. It'll be another hour or so."

"What's her condition, doc?" Q asked, his face a mask of apprehension.

"The main problem is internal bleeding. That's always the hardest with a shot to the abdomen. Fortunately, it was a small-caliber bullet. Her spleen was hit. We've removed it. There's still some bleeding, and the team is working hard to stop it. If we're successful soon, she might make it."

"Jesus Christ, that sounds bad," Q almost shouted.

Phoebe let out a little cry. Her hand fluttered to her mouth, her lips trembled, her knees started to collapse. I grabbed her by the shoulders and took her to a row of seats in front of a wall of glass overlooking the staff parking lot.

"There's still hope, sir. A lot of good people are working hard to save her. She's young and strong. I think we've got a chance. I have to get back now. I'll have the nurse keep you advised."

He left us, and Phoebe started sobbing. Q sat next to her, leaned in, and wrapped his arms around her, cradling her head against his chest.

AT SEVEN A.M., STILL WAITING AT THE HOSPITAL, I CALLED FRANKIE on the cell phone that Alexandra had recently bought her.

"Hey, girl, you waiting at the bus stop?"

"Not yet. It's still early. I got ten more minutes. I'm eating Cheerios and chocolate chips. Red likes Cheerios." Red, Frankie's cat, was not the picky eater that felines have a tendency to be.

"Chocolate chips?" I said. Alexandra had been working on getting her to eat a little healthier with mixed results.

She ignored my comment and said, "You don't have to pick me up from school today."

"Why not?"

"Celia's mom is taking us to the movies to see *Fantastic Beasts*. I can't wait."

"Sounds like fun."

"Yeah. And then we're getting pizza."

"Do you want me to pick you up there?"

"Naw. I think Celia's mom will drive me home." The cellophane rustle of a bag was followed by a mouthful of something that garbled her speech. "Do you think Red would like some chocolate chips?"

"I don't think that's a good idea. Might make her sick."

"Okay. But I don't see how chocolate chips could make anybody sick."

"I'll be waiting for you when you get home."

"Cool. I've got a new kind of Ollie to show you, too."

Another skateboard move. The kid was amazing to watch on the thing.

I hung up, called Marsh, and brought him up to date. I asked if he could take a look around the Black Canary that morning, although I knew it probably wouldn't be open. Locked doors are usually not much of a problem for him. I also asked him if he could find out anything find-out-able about the Children's Network. He said he had meetings all morning but would get out to the area in the afternoon and get somebody digging into the Network right away.

I didn't expect to find much criminal activity going on there. I was sure it was a legitimate and worthy group of people doing their best to help the children. God knows a lot of abandoned kids and runaways in San Francisco needed organizations like it.

But it was necessary information gathering and precaution. Like most investigative work, it was like throwing a dart at a board without a bullseye. You gathered bits of data here and there incrementally, and finally some of the pieces came together and started to make sense.

Or, just as often, not. You ended up with more questions than answers and continued to flail around in the dark.

Hopefully, Marley was competent, despite his personality, and he and his men would quickly identify a suspect. It definitely looked like an act of impulse or passion by an amateur so, at first glance, an eminently solvable case.

But it turned out that that conjecture on my part couldn't have been more premature or more wrong.

SIX

At 8:45 a.m., Dr. Newburgh returned wearing a poker face.

Phoebe immediately jumped to her feet and rushed him. Q and I weren't far behind.

"She's out of surgery. She's in intensive care, so it's still touch and go, but Dr. Ardmore is hopeful. We were able to stop the internal bleeding. But, as the result of an injury to her head when she fell, there was some trauma to her brain and a buildup in fluid. We've induced a coma to allow her brain time to heal."

"Oh my god. A coma?" Phoebe's face blanched, her fingers tugging absently at her lower lip. "For how long?"

"That depends. Time will tell. We're monitoring her closely."

"Can we see her anyway?"

"Not at the moment. As I said, she's in a coma and can't respond. She's hooked up to machines and heavily drugged. The police want to see her, too, ask her questions, of course, but I told them that was impossible at the moment."

I'd noticed several officers lingering in the area. A couple who I'd seen at the nightclub, but I hadn't spotted Marley among them.

"When..." Q asked, but his voice trailed off.

"It's hard to say right now. Perhaps, if you can, go home and get some rest. Leave your contact information with the nurse, and we'll let you know as soon as anything changes."

He patted Phoebe's elbow and offered a half-smile that attempted reassurance, but didn't quite make it, before trudging away.

As we stood there awkwardly, deciding what to do, a young woman approached the nurse's station just across from us, and said, "Could you tell me if it's possible to see Sarah Swan?"

We all turned our heads toward the voice at the same time.

THE FOUR OF US HUDDLED AROUND OUR COFFEES AND TEAS AT A small table in the hospital cafeteria.

Q brought the woman, Ms. Rachel Wambaugh, up to date on the events of the past seven hours.

Both Q and Phoebe knew her, and so did I by name, although I'd only had the dubious pleasure of meeting her mother.

The lion's share of her genetic inheritance must have come from her father because the only resemblance I noticed to Plain Jane Mom was in the tiny ears, and even those seemed more appealing in the daughter. Rachel's looks were classical and in perfect symmetry: high cheekbones, smooth, unblemished skin, eyes the piercingly clear color of the water off Kailua Bay in Hawaii where I'd snorkeled.

Even the sadness in them couldn't diminish her beauty.

Our conversation was stilted because the relationships amongst us and Sarah remained undefined. Supposedly, Rachel was the sister of Sarah's boyfriend.

Where was Christopher? Had he sent his sister in his stead? Possible, but what kind of boyfriend wouldn't bother to rush to the hospital under these conditions? Maybe he didn't know and couldn't be reached.

So, even though no one had clued me as to why she was here, and nobody here had any idea how much I knew about the situation, I asked, "Rachel, are you a close friend of Sarah's?"

She blushed, reached down, wrapped her hand around the Darjeeling tea-filled paper cup, and said, "Yes. My brother has been dating her...but I think they've kind of broken up. But the two of us...Sarah and me, have kind of gotten...to be friends." Her eyes remained on her tea.

I looked over at Phoebe, who was staring at Rachel with an unreadable expression. I felt Q's gaze on me, and I met it. He shook his head subtly back and forth, indicating that I should back off.

I can be a bulldog at times but hadn't intended to press Rachel further. It wasn't the time or place. She was obviously very upset about Sarah, as was everyone else at the table. I wanted to question her and Phoebe and Q, but it would have to wait.

Suddenly, Rachel turned the tables on me. "What is your involvement, Mr. Plank? Are you a friend of Sarah's?"

"I had some private business to discuss with her, and I just happened to show up at the wrong time." *All on account of your dear sweet mother.*

"From what Q tells me, you did your best. Trying to catch whoever did this."

I glanced at Q, who avoided my eyes. Sarah and Rachel had to be good friends for him to call and let her know what had happened in the midst of the chaos.

"I just reacted without thinking. Not quick enough though."

"Thank you, anyway," she said, holding my eyes.

Q rose and said he had an appointment he had to keep but would return in the early afternoon. Phoebe said she was going to stay all day if necessary. Rachel reached across the table and grasped Phoebe's hand.

I gave my card to Phoebe and asked her to call me as soon as she had an update on Sarah's condition or if she needed anything. I bid both women goodbye and left.

It was almost ten a.m., and I had a long day ahead of me.

SEVEN

The *Sweet and Sour* is Dao and Meiying's eighty-five-foot yacht docked a few hundred yards from my own modest little houseboat.

The luxury vessel is made of fiberglass and carbon and finished in teak and stainless steel. It has two Jacuzzis, a pagoda, a game parlor, a sky lounge, and enough state of the art gizmos to beat the band twice.

Dao and I were at the granite-topped bar in the main state-room, sitting on leather barstools staring down at a cribbage board made of polished rosewood.

I looked up at Dao, who was studying his hand. He was in his early sixties, a short, plump man with ruddy cheeks and wide, curious eyes. He'd made a fortune for and with some of the world's top hedge funds and now traded only for himself and a select group of clients. He knew more about money, finance, and economics and the history of it than anybody I'd ever met. And I'd had more than just a few encounters with Wall Street types.

Contrary to popular opinion, they weren't all ethically-chal-lenged greedy savages looking for the quick score and heedless of who got hurt in the process. There were those, sure. Too many of them. But I'd also met some honorable, trustworthy souls, fascinated by the bump and grind and casino action that you can find on Wall Street and precious few other places in American work life. I guess Hollywood offers the same trick or treat thrills, but I'd had less experience with the glitterati.

Within a few minutes of meeting up with Dao, I concluded that Marsh was right about him. There was something bothering my friend. I had actually beaten him the first two games that we played. Not extraordinary, but unusual. His heart and mind were somewhere else and not on the game. This had never happened in the five years we'd been playing regularly.

I do win a consistently small percentage of games, but this was different.

Meiying appeared in the doorway with a tray of won tons and spring rolls and two fine china cups filled with steaming tea that filled the air with an orange and minty scent. She moved to the bar and placed the tea and appetizers between us. I'd brought Frankie along, and she was up on the deck practicing her skateboard moves and, as soon as Meiying returned, would be schooled in the intricacies of dominos.

Dao kept his eyes on the cribbage board, ignoring her presence. Something was definitely wrong. Even after more than thirty years of marriage, he adored her, and whenever she was in the same room as him, his whole affect changed subtly but perceptibly.

She stepped close to me and said, "Plank, you marry Alexandra now."

I frowned at her.

"Do not give me that face. Frankie should have Momma and Poppa. Momma and Poppa who are married to each other."

"Alexandra doesn't even have permanent custody yet."

"No matter. Frankie needs good example now. Plank needs wife."

I knew it was no use arguing with her. I sighed and flashed her my attempt at a cooperative smile.

Her eyebrows arched up until the midlines were touching and her lips pursed. "Otherwise, I know a very nice lady. She Thai. If Alexandra not right," she slapped the table three times with her fore and middle fingers, "and Plank, she is perfect. But if Plank too crazy, then Meiying have very nice Thai. Her name Anong. You know what Anong mean in Thai?"

"No, Meiying, I don't believe I do."

"Mean gorgeous. And Anong is. You want to meet?"

"No."

"Then you marry Alexandra."

I shook my head in amazement at the woman's guileless determination.

She reached over and put her hand over mine. "Listen to Meiying. Men, they not know what they not know. Dao is perfect example." Then she rose and left the room.

I looked at Dao.

He shrugged his shoulders and moved his eyes back to the cribbage board.

I stared at the top of his balding head as he shifted the cards in his hand and examined them as if they held the secret to life.

"What's wrong, Dao?"

His eyes stayed on the cards.

"Dao?"

"Mmmm?" He looked at me for a moment, then handed me the deck to cut. I did so, and he took it back and started dealing.

"What's bothering you?"

"It's nothing."

He finished giving each of us six cards and spread his deal

open between his fingers. He discarded two cards to the crib and waited for me to do the same.

"It's something," I said, and tossed my pair on top of his. I lifted the remainder of the deck roughly in the middle and Dao slipped a card out and placed it face up on top. A Queen of Spades. It seemed significant somehow.

I'm sometimes subject to presentiments. I don't always pay attention to them, but my gut instincts have been tuned and heightened due to the unusual number of dodgy encounters I've experienced, so I do pay attention to these premonitions.

Dao held his hand low, rubbing his fingers absently on the backs of the cards. Usually his play was lightning-quick, but today it was molasses-slow.

"None of my business, of course."

"Yes. True."

He began play and, once again, blew an opportunity to peg and made another thoughtless error, which allowed me to pull ahead and then win the game.

I downed two crisp, delicious spring rolls and followed with a sip of the orange-minty tea in silence.

This too was unusual. Dao was a wily raconteur, always ready with an anecdote or obscure fact whether we were discussing cribbage, local politics, the history of steel factories in Pennsylvania, or the latest Kung Fu movie out of Hong Kong.

After what seemed like an hour, but was probably only five minutes, he turned to me and said, "This is my burden. But perhaps you can offer advice. I am not practiced in the ways of these people, although I understand their nature. They fall outside any predictability patterns." His cheeks flushed red. He clasped his hands tight in a ball and looked over my shoulder into a corner of the room.

Dao is not a man given to exaggeration. Nor is he easily ruffled. He abhors violence, but few situations, no matter how stressful, throw him off his game. My muscles tensed just listening to him and observing his body language.

"Tell me," I said.

"You cannot repeat any of this to Marsh."

"Marsh loves you, Dao." And that's saying something. You could count on the fingers of one hand the people he loved and still have a finger or two left over.

"And I him. But he is a violent man. I know he is skilled, but, even for him...and you, this is far too dangerous."

I had never found the situation in which Marsh couldn't dish out more than he took, but I nodded agreement that I'd keep Dao's secret to myself, at least for now.

"All right. Last spring, do you remember the offering that you were invited to?"

I did. Two or three times a year, Dao had a dinner party on the yacht where he announced one or two particular investment opportunities that he was offering to a select group of rich one-percenters. I'd been to a few of these. They were usually populated by a preponderance of older Asian gentlemen and younger Asian beauties. Money and its unvarying ornamentations. I'd skipped the last couple because Meiying was always trying to set me up with some extraordinarily attractive young woman.

Not that I have anything against extraordinarily attractive young women, but I liked to pick my own dates. I'm funny that way. And besides, Alexandra didn't seem to appreciate my attendance at these functions. She trusted me, sort of, but she'd see seen the stock of talent that Dao attracted, and it would intimidate any woman, no matter how beautiful.

As mentioned, Meiying really likes Alexandra and wants me to marry her. But her prime objective is to get me hitched, no matter the woman.

Dao explained that he'd offered a rather more speculative opportunity than is his custom. He warned the investors of the risk and advised that they invest only a small portion of their assets, an amount they were willing and able to lose. The private offering was in a small pharmaceutical startup called *FutureCare*. They had one drug, a possible breakthrough for Alzheimer's, that was still in FDA trials, but showed great promise. Dao admitted that his own avid interest and emotional connection to the disease that had ravaged his father and his older brother may have clouded his assessment. But he insisted that he'd made the risks clear to the investors, and he had financial statements testifying to their lofty net worths.

A month ago, the FDA had announced disappointing results for the drug in the latest trials. There was a still a chance it might do some people some good, but the side effects—brain clots— were more than disturbing. The offering immediately lost ninety-five percent of its value, and the future of *FutureCare* was precarious, to put a positive spin on it.

Dao and eight of the yacht invitees had invested, and he'd fielded concerned or disappointed calls from several of them, but they'd taken the losses in stride. Dao had made most of them so much money over the years that an occasional bump in the road was just the cost of doing business.

But one of the investors, a new invitee, who had been recommended by an outside financial consultant, had come to the yacht to discuss the situation. Dao was picky about who he invited to these "offering parties" as he called them. He liked working with just a small number of clients, and the amount of money you had wasn't the most important factor in his assessment of a new client. He wanted only stable, seasoned, and reasonable people who were easy to work with, or as easy as rich people can be, used to having things their own way as they are.

He admitted he'd taken on this new client as a favor to his friend and perhaps had not checked him out as thoroughly as is his custom.

Mr. George Liu was a man in his eighties, a successful entrepreneur in the import-export trade. Or at least that was how he represented himself. Dao requires financial statements and then does some follow-up research on his own, and Liu checked out satisfactorily although since he was recommended only a couple of days before the dinner party, Dao didn't investigate to the extent that he normally does. Afterward, he let it slide because he'd gotten a favorable impression of the man.

Five days ago, a young man and three associates arrived on the yacht without benefit of an appointment and insisted upon seeing Dao.

"I didn't like the look of them, but I could see that they were not going away until we met."

"What is that you didn't like?"

"Slick hair. Slick suits. Too much jewelry. The look in the eyes, particularly the man who claimed to be Liu's nephew, Takeshi. His eyes were cold, disdainful. There was no respect in any of the young men.

"...so we stood right here in this room. They refused to sit. And Takeshi told me that I had taken advantage of his uncle. He said that his relative had lost too much money by investing in *Future-Care* and was despondent. Millions of dollars, he claimed."

Dao paused, shook his head, his eyes a little unfocused. After a few seconds, he continued, "I interrupted, telling him that I'd recommended caution and advised that only a tiny percentage of assets should be risked. And, despite the fact that I didn't think I was talking to anyone of financial sophistication, I asked if he'd seen the prospectus and my letter outlining the risks.

"Takeshi stepped close to me and put his nose right up in my face. He towered over me, and I had to look up into his eyes. I must admit that a shiver of fear ran through me. There was nothing but contempt and hatred in his look. I remember his exact words, 'Old man. You cheated my uncle. He is a little crazy.

He doesn't remember things well. I think he suffers from the disease that your drug was supposed to fix. You took advantage and now my family suffers.'

"Max, George Liu seemed as sharp as anyone on the boat that night. There were no signs of trouble." He paused again, curling his fingers around the tea cup, lifted it, then immediately dropped it back down without taking a sip. "Of course, anything is possible. Alzheimer's and dementia are progressive and hard to spot in the early stages..." His voice trailed off as doubts took hold.

"What did he want from you?"

He took a long breath and let it go with a sigh. "A good faith gesture."

"What does that mean?"

"One hundred thousand dollars."

"And he thinks this will make up for the millions that his uncle lost?"

"No. I think he considers it to be an acknowledgement of my culpability and a first step toward retribution. He mentioned that, after my good faith gesture, he would trust me to use my financial skills to pay back what was lost over time."

"How did you react?"

"I was stunned. I asked to speak with George himself, but Takeshi said that the old man was too depressed and confused and angry."

"What did you tell them?"

"I said that if they looked at my letter and the prospectus, they would see my warnings and clear outline of the risks. I told them I wasn't responsible for George Liu's decisions. He had gone well beyond my recommendations and taken an irrational risk."

It sounded like a reasonable defense, but I had the feeling that young Takeshi had found it lacking.

"Takeshi smiled at me, but it was the smile of a dangerous snake. He said that he expected me to hand over one hundred thousand dollars in cash, in one-hundred-dollar bills, in less than a week. At that time, we would discuss further compensation for my treachery." Dao's eyes were the size of saucers as if he still couldn't quite believe what had happened. "Takeshi flung his arms wide and cried that I had betrayed my calling and my clients."

"When is he supposed to pick up the cash?"

"Two days from now. They want to meet here on the boat. At night. They told me to tell no one of our conversation, especially not the police, and that only Meiying and I should await them."

"What did you tell him?"

"Nothing. I was shocked. I could hardly speak. I wanted to throw them off my boat. But there were three of them, young, strong. I was sure they carried weapons under their clothes. I thought about Meiying down below, and an overwhelming fear claimed me. I am ashamed."

He had nothing to be ashamed about, but it was hard to reassure him. Most people, even in this violent country of ours, are unfamiliar with the natural, visceral human responses to threat and intimidation backed by the use of force. In the face of raw violence, the feelings of helplessness and the damage to one's ego, pride, and sense of self can be life-altering.

"Dao, you did the right thing. There's nothing you could have done then and there. Is there anything more you can tell me about these men?"

"They aspire to be Yakuza."

"Why do you say that?"

"I am not an expert, but I have friends in Chinatown who tell me this is a growing problem. Young, aimless men, inspired by myths of the Yakuza. There have been several of these gangs over the years in the city—the Wah Ching and Wo Hop To, along with the Black Dragons operating out of Los Angeles. Some have come and gone, broken up by law enforcement. But new groups always arise."

"Did they indicate they were part of a gang?"

"No. But there were two signs. One, tattoos hidden under the clothes—"

"Tattoos are pretty common, unfortunately, among the young now—"

"Not like these. Takeshi, before he left, rolled up his sleeve all the way to his shoulder and showed me an Oni Mask tattoo on his bicep. He flexed his muscle, making the demon with a club tattooed there ripple."

"Wow. This guy has watched too many Samurai movies, eh?"

"He is familiar with Yakuza customs. The Oni are punishers and shape shifters, and they inflict disease, insanity, and death to the wicked. They terrorize and exact retribution."

"So he fancies himself a Yakuza?"

"He probably is a member or leader of a gang based upon Yakuza rites and traditions. Likely no direct connection to actual Yakuza, but I cannot know for sure."

"You said there were two reasons."

"The other was also tattoos hidden by the clothes. This is typical Yakuza. The tattoos, often extending over the entire body, are usually not carried onto visible areas. Thus, the face and neck and hands and wrists are usually tattoo-free so that gang members cannot be easily identified."

That made sense. No reason to make it easier for the cops and your enemies.

"Let's get the police involved. You should not meet with these jerks."

Dao shook his head back and forth vigorously. "No. No. They said I should tell no one. That if I did, my family would face the wrath of the demon."

"You're kidding. He actually said, 'wrath of the demon'?"

Dao nodded grimly.

"Well, you're not going to be on this boat when they arrive—"

"I have to be. Meiying will be in danger and—"

"If you give them this 'good faith gesture,' they won't stop. They've admitted it. You'll be theirs. This is blackmail. They are threatening Meiying."

Dao sighed, gripped his hand around the tea cup and closed his eyes.

"I don't know..." he said, his voice trailing off.

"Lookit, maybe they're just bluffing. We need to find out more about them. I wish you'd told me sooner, but let me see what I can find out quickly."

I put my hand on his shoulder and squeezed it, and he opened his eyes and stared bleakly into my face.

It pained me to see this good, gentle, kind man so tormented.

These Yakuza wannabes could stand to learn a lesson about picking on somebody their own size.

EIGHT

I was sitting on the back deck of *Acapella Blues*, sipping Italian Roast with a dash of half and half, staring out onto the tranquil Bay waters and Treasure Island in the distance, which made me think of Poe and his casino and what he might be up to. No good, I was sure, but I hadn't had any contact with him since the events of Frankie's case more than nine months ago. I was hoping for that streak of luck to continue for the rest of my life.

My mind was a jumble of conflicting thoughts and emotions around the events at the Black Canary along with Dao's predicament. I was waiting to hear back from Marsh.

The phone, sitting on the table beside me, rang, and I snatched it up.

But instead of Marsh's familiar dulcet tones, a woman's grating voice blasted my ear drums.

"What on God's green earth has been going on, Mr. Plank?"

It didn't take me more than a couple of seconds to realize my new client had her panties in a bunch.

"Good day to you too, Mrs. Wambaugh."

"Nonsense. I understand you witnessed Sarah's shooting?"

"I was there, yes."

"And you spoke with my daughter?"

"Right again."

"I don't approve."

"Pardon?"

"I didn't authorize you to speak with either of my children."

The woman definitely had a bad case of Mom-entitlemen-mania.

"Surely you jest."

"None of your smart-aleck comments. This is too serious. Too upsetting."

"What, precisely, are you worried about?" I was pretty sure it wasn't a deep concern about Sarah's health.

"Well, I do feel sorry about Ms. Swan's injury. Nevertheless, it's not surprising, considering her character. What I am concerned about is the effect of all this on poor Christopher and Rachel, who, I've learned, has been taken in by that woman's counterfeit charms."

I could almost hear the gnashing and grinding of the matriarchal teeth on the other end of the line.

"You didn't know your daughter and Sarah had become friends?"

"Certainly not. If I had, I would have put a stop to it."

Wow.

"I still don't know what you have against Sarah. It would be nice to have a clue as to why you so despise her."

"Don't tell me, have you too been deceived? I should have known that—"

"I've haven't yet had the chance to meet her formally. I heard her sing, which, you'll be sorry to hear, she does splendidly."

She mumbled something that I couldn't make out and then said, "I think, for the time being, I want to put your services on hold. I don't want you bothering my children, and with Ms.

Swan in the hospital in critical condition, it would be unseemly for you to investigate her any further. I will let you know if your services are needed again once the situation becomes clearer."

The word unseemly really hit me like she'd plucked the wrong guitar string.

"Do you remember what I told you when I agreed to work for you?"

There was a long pause as she was either trying to recall my words or, having remembered, was letting steam build up in that angry, self-righteous teapot dome of hers.

"I'm telling you that you'll be hearing from my attorneys should you proceed in this bull-headed—"

My phone signaled another call, and I interrupted her, "Must be going, ma'am. Have a pleasant day."

I clicked her off and smiled as I sensed the blood-curdling scream that I was sure had exploded from somewhere high atop a hill in Atherton.

MARSH AND I SAT OUTSIDE ON THE DECK OF OUR FRIEND BO Fiddler's restaurant, the Rusty Root, not too far from my boat. The air was rife with a briny sea scent, along with the smell of suntan lotion and fish, both fresh and rotting. A pair of seagulls perched on the railing just a few feet from our platters of cod, potatoes, and slaw. They were acting nonchalant, their spring-loaded heads bobbing this way and that, pretending like they cared about something else other than stealing our lunch.

"You're kidding?" Marsh said.

"Nope."

"He flexed his bicep, rippling a demon?"

"Sounds pretty impressive. He must have practiced that in the mirror for days before hauling it out to show Dao."

"Undoubtedly a budding DeNiro. What do you think we should do?"

"Kill them."

Marsh is a no-nonsense kind of guy, and his first resort is often most people's very last.

"I think we might hold that option off for just a little while."

"Why?"

"Do you think we should let Dao meet with them with us as backup or should we just dispense altogether with the middleman?"

"Not enough information to make a decision."

"What do you suggest then, other than murder?"

"Dao nixed getting the police involved?"

"He's worried about Meiying. I'm sure he thinks that no matter how the cops handle it, they'll still be vulnerable."

"Understandable. But we don't know what we're dealing with. How many of them there are and, really, how dangerous? Do they actually have skills or are they just play-acting amateurs. Let me look into this George Liu fellow see if there's anything about him that gives us a clue."

"How about his nephew, Takeshi?"

"We'll run him too, although he may not be an actual nephew, and Takeshi may not be his real name." Marsh forked a potato, gave it a wary stare, and placed it in his mouth.

"We've got less than two days until the meeting."

"I should have something by tonight." Marsh's ability to gather info never failed to surprise. He had sources and contacts throughout the city and world, and there was always seemed to be somebody in his network with his finger on the pulse of the never-ending nefarious activities happening on the streets of San Francisco. Plus, he had a couple of computer gurus extraordinaire on the payroll, including the comely Portia, a preternaturally talented hacker, who had helped with Frankie's case.

"Mrs. Wambaugh wants me off the case."

"Can't blame her. But you're not going to comply, of course." Marsh knew my nature, a blind-to-the-consequences doggedness once I had my teeth clenched to the bone. He thought I was nuts, a Knight-Errant, a regular foolish Don Quixote, but he accepted my little peccadillos, just as I did his.

I shrugged.

He frowned.

"You have any clue yet as to why or who tried to kill the singer?"

"None whatsoever. That's all I can say, despite Mrs. Wambaugh's claims, is that, without ever having spoken to her, I like her and all the people around her."

"So she's hot?"

"Marsh, she's in critical condition in the hospital."

"Doesn't affect the nature of her basic hotness."

"My feelings have nothing to do with her looks."

"But I bet she's hot."

I sighed. "Yes, she is attractive. But her singing is so compelling, and her bandmates and friends and the people at the Black Canary love her so much, that you can't help but get a good vibe. If she doesn't make it, a lot of people are going to be devastated."

"Good vibrations lead to excitations as Brian Wilson would say," Marsh murmured.

I rolled my eyes. "Anything to tell me about your trip to the Black Canary and the Children's Network?"

"The Black Canary was closed, but I didn't have to sneak in. The bartender was inside and let me in. We had a nice chat. Alice is a tough butch. But you're right, she's one of those who loves Sarah Swan. Didn't have a single negative thing to say. She was broken up about the shooting. The cops had already grilled her, of course, and she was suspicious of me at first, but my innate charm won out, and by the end, we were good buddies. She wants to go out with me."

"You're kidding?"

"Few women, hetero or less, can resist. Unfortunately for them, what they have I don't need."

"She's attracted to you?"

"Of course. But she just wants to be friends. We have some of the same views about the gay scene here and, surprise, she's interested in martial arts and kabuki. She's meeting me at a gym downtown next week."

"Good to hear you're making friends. But was she helpful at all regarding possible suspects?"

"A bit. The one person she was a little suspicious of was her boyfriend, Christopher, the youngest member of the Wambaugh clan. She said Sarah had broken up with him and, from what she understood, he was pretty ripped up about it."

"Losing a woman like Sarah would more than hurt."

"Because she's such a good singer and so sweet," Marsh said with a grin on his face.

"And tres hot," I said, then added, "What did she think of him?"

"Alice didn't know him well. But she thought he was immature for his age, shy and adolescent in some ways. She said he was cute but wondered why Sarah had bothered with him."

"That it?"

"Yes. Alice let me wander around. She showed me where the shooting happened, and I checked out the back alleys for a while. I visited the Children's Network, but different people were on duty from the night you entered. Everything seemed pretty okay there. They seemed to be doing what they're supposed to be doing. But Portia came up with a couple of interesting tidbits—"

A seagull's bony beak snatched a chunk of my fish and lifted away at the same moment that Marsh's snapped a fingertip at its breast. It screeched and flapped wildly, stalling in mid-air above our table for a moment, before regaining its composure and veering away.

"Least he won't be back any time soon," Marsh said.

"I wonder if Bo will still make me pay?" I said, hoping for a break from my friend and the owner of this fine establishment.

"Likely. So Portia hacked their personnel files, and it turns out that little Christopher has volunteered there on and off for several years. And Sarah is also on the list of volunteers. Looks like she's been spending some free time there for the past year or so."

"Now that is interesting."

"And since you know how I feel about coincidences, I'd say we need to take a good, hard look at the young Wambaugh."

When it came to crime, or evil, or unethical behavior, Marsh didn't put much stock in chance. He believed that a preponderance, or even sometimes a modicum, of circumstantial evidence was usually enough to convict, damn the legal system.

"In this case, I agree."

"And that's not all. Although they've tried to bury the news, the Children's Network was sued several years back by two kids who stayed there. They claimed physical and sexual abuse. The charges were eventually dismissed and the boys' stories discredited, but still."

"Was Christopher volunteering there at the time?"

"Unclear. Portia is sifting through the records, and she's trying to see if she can locate any internal or secret documents or settlement papers regarding the child abuse cases. I've got her plate pretty full, but I'll tell her to focus on this today."

"Anything else?"

"We should find out who else knew you were working for Mrs. Wambaugh and investigating Sarah Swan."

"I don't understand."

"Do you think that it's just a coincidence that someone tried to kill her the night you happened to visit the Black Canary for the first time?"

"I hadn't thought about it."

"That's why you need me."

"So the killer wanted me there? That doesn't make—"

"Probably not. More likely, your involvement panicked somebody. They didn't want you talking to Sarah. So they decided to get rid of her. I'd imagine they wanted to do it before you showed up, but since you were so quick about it..."

"I don't know. It's a leap."

"Less of a leap than swallowing the idea that your presence and the shooting were mere happenstance."

I knew he was right. And his information about the link between Christopher and Sarah and the Children's Network was disturbing.

"I guess we'd better find Christopher and have a heart-to-heart."

"Mom's not going to like it."

"I think it's going to be awfully hard to please Mom any way you look at it, so I don't expect to try."

"Wow."

"Mom spelled upside down."

"Precisely."

NINE

I was at Alexandra's house in Pacific Heights waiting for Frankie to come home from the movies when Phoebe finally returned my call.

She quickly brought me up to date.

"That's good news then."

"She's still in serious condition."

"That's better than critical."

"Still in a coma. They don't know when they'll bring her out of it yet. Maybe as much as another week or so. But the doctor said all her vital signs have stabilized, and her chances have improved significantly over the past few hours."

"So she's going to make it."

"God, I hope so. I don't know what I'd do..." She paused, gathering her emotions.

I waited until she regained her composure. "Sarah's lucky to have such a caring friend."

"I'm the lucky one. Without Sarah...I don't know where I'd be. She took a chance on me, hired me after..." She paused, took a deep breath, then continued, "It's just that she helped out at a very bad time in my life."

Once again, I contrasted Mrs. Wambaugh's assessment of Sarah to the people who knew her best and couldn't reconcile the competing versions. But since Mom was not exactly a sympathetic witness, I was nearing the point where I could completely discount her view as self-interested. But I really needed to talk to Sarah and hoped I'd get the chance soon.

"Do you know where Sarah lives?"

"Sure. She has an apartment on 33rd Avenue, near Golden Gate Park. She loves that park. Loves to have tea in the Japanese Gardens."

"She lives alone?"

"Yes. While she was dating Christopher, he actually wanted her to move in with him. She couldn't believe it because they'd only dated for a few weeks and she was never serious about him. She said she gave him no encouragement in that direction."

"How upset?"

"Just typical when someone you love doesn't feel the same way. He didn't get violent or anything. It was always kind of a one-sided relationship anyway. She thought he was cute, like a puppy. But too immature to have a real relationship with. Plus, there was Mrs. Wambaugh. I never met her, but I guess she hated Sarah. Sarah couldn't believe what a bitch she was. Since Christopher didn't really stand up to her, I think that kind of did in their relationship in the end."

"What about Christopher? Where does he live? And Rachel, too."

She hesitated, cleared her throat, blew her nose. "Well, until recently, they lived together in a condo in the Embarcadero. Supposed to be total luxury with amazing Bay views. Sarah says it's unbelievable since neither one of them makes much money. I guess their mom picks up the tab. But Christopher moved out a few weeks ago. Sarah said he's living temporarily with his mother."

After telling her that I'd probably be at the hospital sometime tomorrow, I got off the phone knowing that first thing in the morning I'd be heading out to Atherton to see how the ultra-wealthy lived.

My thoughts were interrupted by a call from London.

"How are ya, big fella?"

"I love it when you call me big fella."

"I've never called you big fella before."

"That wasn't you?"

"Funny guy."

"That's me. A laugh riot."

"How's Frankie?"

"Out seeing *Fantastic Beasts*."

"Pardon me?"

"It's a movie."

"I'll bet it is. Are you two doing okay without me?"

"No."

"Having trouble knowing what to do as a surrogate parent?"

"No. Thanks to Frankie, who's amazing. She pretty much takes care of herself. I just give her some check-in support. But I've got this new case that has me bent out of shape."

"Nothing unusual."

"Easy for you to say."

"Tell me about it." I did. Alexandra has an analytical mind and a nose for research and ferreting out salient facts nurtured by her twenty years as an investigative journalist. She sometimes picks up on things that I miss.

"Mmmm. Has to be about money."

"And probably family secrets."

"What about the father?"

"Marsh says he's kind of a ghost. Has been for the past ten, fifteen years."

"I'd find out more about him."

"Him and about a half-dozen others, including Sarah, if she recovers and I can talk to her."

"Remember how confounding Frankie's case was."

"You're right. This one is child's play so far compared to that."

"Find about the father," she repeated.

"Max! That was so cool…"

Frankie burst through the front door and unleashed a fusillade of words about the movie. It sounded like J.K. Rowling was going to continue to be the richest woman in England for a while longer.

I told Frankie that Alexandra was on the phone, and she snatched the receiver away from me. As she began describing the movie, I went to the kitchen to put the frozen pizza I picked up for dinner in the oven.

While I listened to Frankie's excited chatter and waited for the oven to warm, I added the missing patriarch of the family to the growing list of prospects I needed to talk to.

I also flashed on a notion that would kill two birds with one stone. I was going to ask Meiying to come and stay here with Frankie for a couple of days, which would free me to pursue leads, and also get her off Dao's boat so Marsh and I could prepare for Takeshi and his gang's return.

All in all. Things were looking up. I had a plan. I had a pizza in the oven.

Alexandra and Frankie seemed happy with each other and with me.

Things might turn to fecal matter by tomorrow, but for right now, life was peachy keen.

TEN

Early the next morning, after walking Frankie to the bus
stop, it took me around an hour to drive out to the most
expensive zip code in the country. Five square miles of
ultra-exclusive, woodsier-than-thou real estate nestled in the
heart of San Mateo, near Stanford University. You'd have to look
far and wide, and you'd end up on a fool's errand, to find a place
that you could spend more money for a house than Atherton.

I felt a little richer in spirit if not in reality just driving
through. Life's possibilities seemed to open up. The sun overhead
was struggling to peek through a layer of gray clouds, but I was
sure that it would burst through here first.

I was hoping that Phoebe's information was correct, and I
wasn't on my own fool's errand. I had no desire for a tête-à-tête
with Mrs. Wambaugh. I was hoping that Christopher was holed
up in the bosom of his family and that his mother would allow
him to talk to me, and if she didn't, then being a fully grown
twenty-four-year-old man, he'd make his own decision. In other
words, I was hoping he wasn't another man child.

I rounded a wide curve lined with white oaks and a smattering of soaring redwoods and spotted a mailbox that corresponded with the number I had.

The driveway was made of cobbled stone. It was long and twisty and snaked through a thicket of more redwoods and cedar and pine. Beautiful brick planters, hundreds of them, filled with bright blue and yellow and pink flowers of all sorts lined the driveway. It had to be someone's full time job just to care for and water the things.

Beauty has its price. and in Atherton, they can afford to pay it.

After a long trek, just when I thought that the driveway might turn out to be a bridge to nowhere, it finally opened up into a wide shamrock-shaped parking area fronting a sprawling single-story house framed in redwood. There were two other buildings to the north of the main structure. One was a fancy barn that looked to be a horse stable. I guessed by the fact that there were a lot of hay bales about and two lustrous brown horses grazing nearby.

The other structure was a large two-story cottage, probably guest or servant quarters or some such combination. The architectural style was a mix of California contemporary with touches of French Colonial. Windows and wood and red brick melded agreeably with the landscape. Old money spent decorously.

A familiar sound drew my eyes back toward the main house. The thwack of a racket smacking an air-filled rubber ball of jaundiced hue.

I couldn't see the tennis court as it was hidden by the house and the thick trees. I also couldn't see the pool, which I was sure was there despite not hearing any tell-tale splashes. My years of investigative work have fine-tuned my understanding of human nature and its predictability.

I got off my bike, parked it beneath a redwood, and ambled along a crushed stone pathway beside the house.

There it was, a glistening rectangular-shaped pool with a

Polaris pool sweep riding its blue-green surface, spouting water like a baby porpoise. Attached to the pool was an elevated spa framed in red brick, and behind that was a kind of Roman atrium structure with benches and tables and couches enough to seat a hundred people. Also the biggest built-in BBQ I'd ever seen with enough grill area to feed burgers to the third infantry.

The tennis court, or rather courts, were located about fifty yards behind the backyard and pool area. The property had to be at least five acres, perhaps more. Behind the standard chain-link fencing, a man with medium-length, wavy, red hair wearing tennis whites lay crouched and staring at an odd-looking machine. A white-topped oblong-shaped bowl filled with yellow tennis balls sat above a red plastic base that read *Lobster* on the side and front. The device looked nothing like a lobster, and I wondered why the marketeers chose that name.

It looked like two irregularly shaped polyhedrons made of plastic and mashed together. But I guess it would be hard to fit that description on the side of the device and even harder to market it in a catchy way.

Every few seconds, a ball would shoot out of Lobster, and the red-haired man would smack it with authority.

The door to the courts was open, and I took that as a welcome sign. Christopher Wambaugh was so involved with the Lobster that he didn't notice me until I spoke. By that time, I was less than ten feet away from him.

"Nice stroke," I said.

Startled, he dropped his racket.

"Sorry."

A tennis ball hit him in the thigh. He took a step back, stumbled, staring at me in surprise or horror or fear.

But I'm not such a bad guy once you get to know me, so I pushed forward.

"I'm Max Plank. You're Christopher, right?"

He was a good-looking kid, more pretty than handsome, although a little wan. Very white, which made his orange-red hair stand out. He had wary green eyes and was slim and soft with thin arms and spindly legs.

"Who are you?"

"Max Plank," I repeated. He hadn't heard of me. I'm always shocked by the number of people unfamiliar with my oeuvre.

He reached down and picked up his tennis racket. A ball whizzed between us, just missing my elbow.

"What do you want?"

"Just to chat. I'm a friend of your mother's. And of Sarah's."

"Sarah?"

"Sarah Swan. Your girlfriend."

"We broke up."

"Still. You know what happened to her?"

He looked away. Another ball shot by, slamming against the fence behind us.

Christopher turned, walked over to Lobster, and flipped a switch. The low humming sound that I hadn't been aware of stopped. It was quiet save for the chattering of little birds and the sound the soft breeze made moving through the trees. The scent of pine needles with an underlay of chlorine from the pool filled my nose.

He stayed near the machine, studying me with watchful eyes. I kept my gaze steady on him but gave him time. Finally, he said, "Why are you here?"

"Actually, I'm working for your mom. She had me investigating Sarah, and I was there the night she was shot."

"Bullshit," he said.

"Okay. Why am I here?"

He frowned. "My mother did not hire you. She wouldn't..." He hesitated, looked away, trying to make sense of things. "She couldn't, wouldn't dare..."

"She did and does, Christopher. Why would I make that up?"

"Shit," he said, sounding more exasperated or frustrated than angry.

"Why did she hire you? What the hell is wrong with everyone?"

I wasn't sure what he meant by that, but I plunged forward. "She hired me because she didn't trust Sarah. Your mother thought she was taking advantage of you."

"We broke up...she broke up with me."

"Did you tell your mother that?"

He closed his eyes, gripping the tennis racket until the knuckles on his right hand turned red.

A little girl laughed somewhere nearby. A big splash coming from another pool in the house to the north of this one.

"Were you upset with Sarah?"

"Of course. Wouldn't you be?"

I just looked at him, offering no relief.

"Have you been to see her in the hospital?"

"We broke up," he said, firmly, as if that explained his behavior. All emotion and feeling erased in an instant.

"Had to be recently, right? Just in the past few weeks? So you don't care at all that somebody shot her, almost killed her?"

"Of course I care. I talk to Rachel every day. She says no one can see Sarah. She's in a coma. I don't know whether she wants to see me or not anyway, but I'll go to the hospital as soon as Rachel tells me I can."

"Where were you that night she was shot?"

I'd startled him again. "So that's why you're here? Because you think I tried to kill her?"

"I'm talking with anybody and everybody connected to Sarah. Trying to figure out who had a motive to want her dead. At this point, I don't suspect anyone, but everyone is a suspect."

"What are you some kind of fancy P.I. or something?"

"Or something," I said. I don't like to think of myself as fancy. Perhaps a little whimsical at times.

"The cops have already been here asking questions. I don't know why I should talk to you."

"Detective Marley?

He dipped his chin a smidge in response.

"How'd you like him?"

He wrinkled his face in displeasure.

"Yes, he's an acquired taste, and an asshole."

"Still, he asked all the questions that you've asked."

"But I'm a lot nicer guy, right?"

"Jeez," he muttered.

"What do you do?" I asked, one of my out-of-the-blue questions. You'd think it would be part of a grand strategy to get at the truth, but I'm just a curious guy and was wondering what a hyperspoiled young man like this one did with his time.

"What do you mean?"

"What do you do to occupy yourself. I mean," I waved a hand all round me, "you've got all this, but it has nothing to do with you. You didn't earn it. You just found yourself in the right womb. So, do you have a job?"

"You don't know shit about me. I don't have to tell you anything about myself."

"I guess not. But I'll find out anyway. Us fancy P.I.'s have our ways of finding out."

"Screw you."

"Lookit, kid, I'm just trying to find out who shot Sarah. I know you must still have feelings for her, even though you're hurt. Why not cooperate with me? I'm good at what I do. Will you help me? Let's find the shooter and put him where he belongs."

He gave me the proverbial long, silent stare, but then something broke, he shrugged his shoulders and said, "Mom, really hired you?"

"She sure did."

"Shit, she's too much."

I nodded. No point in restating the obvious. I didn't think he was a momma's boy, but it had to be a struggle maintaining your independence with someone as overly controlling as Mrs. Wambaugh, and in the lap of this kind of luxury.

"When was the last time you were at the Children's Network offices down near the Black Canary?"

He looked surprised, his forehead wrinkled up, trying to puzzle something out.

"You volunteer there, right? How often are you there? Were you there the night Sarah was shot?"

He opened his mouth. Shut it. His face flushed red. He rubbed the back of his hand across his face. "I…if you're trying to accuse me of—"

"Simple questions, Christopher. You're going to have to answer them sooner or later. If not to me, then the police."

"This is bull. I haven't been over there for weeks. Haven't had time to volunteer. I didn't have anything to do with Sarah's—"

"Busy guy, eh?" I didn't wait for his answer. "How about your father?"

His eyes widened, and his face tightened. A bit of a shock that one. Wrong question or the wrong time.

He was saved by a shrill bell.

"Plank! Christopher!" Someone was yelling from inside the house, and it didn't take me more than a millisecond to determine who that was.

"Stop! Right now! Wait. Wait right there."

We both turned and looked and caught Mrs. Wambaugh tearing out of the sliding doors fronting the back of the house, her long aqua silk gown trailing high behind her. She looked a bit disheveled, her hair not perfectly coiffed, her makeup not yet applied. I doubted she ever let the world see her this way, but a threat to her family left her sense of propriety in the dust.

Neither of us said a thing while we waited and watched her stride purposefully toward us. When she was mere feet from me, she gave me a stern narrow-eyed look of disdain and barked, "How dare you?"

"Good day to you too, Mrs. Wambaugh."

Her face turned even redder. Steam escaped her ears. I kid you not. Okay. Maybe I just imagined it, but it seemed real at the time. "Who gave you permission to trespass on my property?"

I looked around, exchanged a glance with Christopher, who looked alarmed and maybe a little sympathetic toward my plight. "Well, would you believe I was taking a ride on my bike and found myself in this idyll and remembered you live here and felt it would be rude to not stop and say hello."

More figurative steam shooting out of her ears. "How dare you?"

"You already said that and—"

"Mom, did you hire this man?"

That pulled her up short. "Christopher, I'd appreciate it if you left us alone and went inside. We will discuss this later."

"Mom—"

"Christopher," she literally shrieked.

"Damn it," he muttered, but to my surprise, he turned and trudged off, disappearing inside the same sliding doors that had unleashed the shrew.

"Does your husband live here?"

Her face froze in a rictus. I waited for it to defrost.

"Neither my husband, nor any other member of my family, is any of your concern. I told you that you were no longer working for me. If I catch you anywhere near my property again, I will call the local police, who know me well and will be most eager to deal with a problem like you on my behalf. Do you understand?"

I spun on my heel and left her there sputtering.

"Do you understand?" she shouted again.

"And that goes for my son and daughter. Stay away from them!"

When I got back to my motorcycle, I sat for a moment contemplating the nature of the things I'd learned.

I only knew two things for sure. First, whether Christopher Wambaugh was a momma's boy or not, his mother had a firm hold on him. And, secondly, Mrs. Wambaugh had something to hide. Maybe more than one something.

I switched on the Ducati, and it roared to life, humming like a big cat between my legs. I felt like I was on the trail of something big and wild and bad, and I intended to ride its tail no matter where it led.

ELEVEN

We stood at the foot of the bed and looked at Sarah's limp form, pale and ever-so-fragile, a breathing tube in her nose, an IV snaking out of her arm. A computer screen kept track of what was happening inside her, monitoring blood pressure, heart function, and brain activities of various sorts. A continuous clicking sound accompanied the visual aids like a single cicada snapping its wings.

It was a private room with a bathroom in intensive care. I could see the stainless-steel sink and the pristine white elevated toilet seat through the half-open door. Above the bed was a watercolor in shades of blue and green—a river, a meadow, a waterfall cascading down into a placid pool. A small television opposite the bed and above our heads was tuned to the financial news network. Ticker tape stock quotes reeled by in silence. At the far end of the room, a window looked out onto the emergency room parking lot.

It smelled like hospital. Antiseptic, medicinal, with a slightly sour scent.

Sarah was still in a coma. She looked like a frozen angel,

sleeping peacefully. Snow White waiting for Prince Charming's wakening kiss.

She hadn't opened her eyes or uttered a word in more than two days. No one, including the police, had been able to question her.

There was an officer in the waiting area with a Krispy Creme donut and a coffee reading *Vanity Fair* magazine.

After a few seconds of us standing awkwardly around the bed, a bell rang out in the corridor and someone cried out in pain. Nurse Sadie glanced nervously at us and said, "I think it's best if you leave now. Her condition is stable. Nothing to do now until the doctors decide it's time to bring her out of the coma."

We thanked the nurse for allowing us the brief visit and followed her out the door of Sarah's room.

PHOEBE AND I HUDDLED OVER COFFEE AND TOASTED BLUEBERRY muffins in the hospital cafeteria.

"Do you think she's going to be okay?"

"Yes," Doctor Plank said, confidently.

"She looked so pale. And thin. Maybe it's my imagination. But she must have lost twenty pounds in two days."

At the table closest to us, a man and woman were gripping hands, touching foreheads, and reciting the Lord's prayer in unison.

Phoebe gave them a sidelong glance. A tear escaped her right eye, trailing down her cheek.

"She's going to recover. From what everybody tells me, she's strong. It'll just take a little while. Before you know it, she'll be out of that coma."

She nodded her head repeatedly, wanting to believe me, trying to convince herself that I was right.

I reached out and patted her hand. "Now that it's been a couple of days, do you remember anything else about that evening? Anything unusual? Anything Sarah might have said or done. Anyone she talked to?"

She glanced back over at the praying couple who had finished whispering and were just sitting there, foreheads touching, hands tightly clasped, eyes closed.

"I don't know...I've been so frazzled...but I have thought about it. The police asked me to try and...to remember anything that might help..."

She stopped, took a deep breath. I let her take her time.

A little boy shouted, "I want chocolate pudding now!" His mother grabbed his wrist and yanked downward, and he squealed and burst into tears. She dragged him out of the cafeteria, an expression of stoic resolve on her face.

"It's nothing, I'm sure. Stupid. I don't even know why I thought of it."

"What's nothing?" Nothing is never nothing and sometimes turns out to be quite something.

Said the Mad Hatter to Alice.

Phoebe drummed her fingers on the table, glanced at me, then twisted her cheek to the side, frowned, and said, "Flowers."

"Flowers?"

"Red roses."

I looked at her and waited.

"Sarah doesn't like them. I don't know why. Something about them bothers her. A couple of times fans have sent them, and she'd never keep them. She'd either give them to me or somebody else or dump them in the trash."

"What does this have to do with—"

"Twenty red roses in a box were delivered to the club for Sarah that afternoon. I didn't remember until last night. It wasn't anything important. Not shocking or anything, other than everybody kind of knows this odd quirk about Sarah—this time it seemed to bother her even more than before. She seemed a little freaked out about it. Before, roses just seemed to leave her cold. This time it was more than that. Hard to describe, but it was really noticeable."

"Who sent them?"

"I don't know. There was a note, but it just said, 'Break a Leg,' and was signed Love, your admirer, or something like that."

"So it might have just been a fan who didn't know about her aversion to red roses."

"Probably. That's why I said it was nothing."

"But it's not what you think?"

"I don't know what I think. Not for sure. I just thought it was a little strange. 'Break a Leg'?"

"Doesn't that just mean good luck in show business? You say the opposite thing to the performer because wishing them good luck might backfire. It's a superstitious thing, right?"

"Yes. But it's more used in theater. I don't think I've ever heard it said to Sarah before. Never been said to me. Maybe people do, but I thought it was a little off. And then that ardent admirer sign-off. It sounds like something from an old movie made back in the forties. I know, it all sounds so innocent. And I'm sure it is. I just—"

"What did Sarah think?"

"She thought it was weird, too. Especially the ardent admirer bit. And the fact that there were twenty roses."

"That does seem an odd number."

"Yes. It's always been a dozen or one. We couldn't figure out why twenty. We thought maybe the fan had seen her nineteen times before and this was going to be his...or her twentieth. Who knows?"

"What happened to the flowers?"

"I don't know. Sarah probably gave them to somebody."

"It might be nothing, but I'd like to see that note. Can you ask around the club and see if anybody knows what happened to the flowers and the package they came in?"

She pursed her lips and said, "Yes, I'm going in later today to get music for a show this weekend. I'll ask Alice and the boys."

The praying couple got up from their table and, holding hands, walked slowly, with a palpable sense of doom on their faces, out of the cafeteria.

Phoebe's cell phone rang, and she took it out of her side pocket.

"Chaz," she said, letting out a long, slow breath.

She held the phone tight to her ear and started fidgeting with her left hand, picking up a salt shaker and tapping it on the table while listening.

Chaz was angry. I couldn't hear every word, but he was yelling and mentioned "that damn hospital" a couple of times. He mentioned something about his dinner and wasn't she tired of doctors and hospitals. Sarah tried to protest a couple of times, mumbling, "Chaz, Sarah...and Chaz, you don't understand...and sorry, Chaz...I'll be home tonight."

I didn't like his tone. I didn't like her submissiveness. I wanted to reach through the phone and ring Chaz's neck.

When she hung up, her face was flushed red with shame. "Sorry," she murmured.

Now I was ashamed. "Phoebe, have you been sick?"

"Yeah. I'm in remission. Breast cancer. They say they think they got it all. I finished chemotherapy a few weeks ago."

She smiled shyly, reached up and patted her bald head, "I always wanted to go bald anyway. Now I know what it feels like. Doesn't look half-bad, does it?"

"Half-bad? Phoebe, you're gorgeous."

She smiled at me. "You're a nice man, Max."

"Shhh. Don't let anybody hear you say that. Not good for my reputation."

She laughed.

"What's with Chaz?"

Her smile vanished. "He's okay. Just…kind of tired of doctors and hospitals. It was tough on him having to help me while I was being treated. He doesn't know why I have to come to the hospital so much for Sarah. He likes me home at night." She laughed again, but it wasn't a happy laugh. "I guess like most men he likes his dinner on the table and his woman in the kitchen at night."

I wondered if Chaz was a really old dude. That might give him an excuse for his lame attitudes. I felt for Chaz, having to put up with all the muss and fuss of Phoebe's cancer.

Anybody named Chaz had a lot to apologize for in any case.

Phoebe studied my face and picked up on my thoughts. "But he's a good guy overall. I don't know what I would have done without him while I was being treated. He and Sarah were always there. Q, too, in his own way."

I nodded, let it go.

I'd learned over the years that it's not a good idea to criticize a partner or spouse, no matter what the situation looks like from the outside.

People have all sorts of reasons for staying together, healthy or not. Dysfunction takes many forms, not all of them godawful.

Max Plank, therapist-at-large.

TWELVE

Q took a sip of Blanton's Single Barrel Kentucky Whiskey from the cut glass tumbler and murmured, "Hmmm mmmm." He lifted the cigarette, that I'd just watched him roll with panache, to his lips and breathed in before blowing it out to his left, away from me. "Sometimes, Plank, it's the little things that make life worth living, despite all the big shit being fucked up."

We were sitting at a little table in a dark corner of the Double Musky Inn. A big candle, bubbling and cratering in the middle of the table, lit up the craggy corners of his fascinating face.

There was a platter of oysters in the middle of the table, and one of *Muskies* famous half-pound burgers with caramelized onions dripping onto a French roll in front of each of us.

Although oysters, cigarettes, and whiskey don't float my boat, I had to agree with him. The burger and the chocolate malt next to it provided a close proximity of the thrill he was feeling.

The Double Musky is one of those true American hybrids, with a menu impossible to classify, but if you couldn't find something to satisfy your tastes you were probably a vegan and even vegans had deep fried plantains to resort to. The portions were big enough to satisfy a polar bear just waking up from winter hibernation.

Q had just finished telling me about his real name, Quentin Quest. He said the name made no sense, especially for a black man. He figured the last name probably belonged to some slave plantation owner and he attributed his given name to his mother's love for alliteration. She was a poor housemaid for most of her life and wouldn't have recognized the term, but she loved nonsense poetry and rhyming, and was a big fan of Dr. Seuss.

Q lifted his whiskey toward me and said, "To Sarah." I tapped my malt against his tumbler and nodded. He gave my malt a funny look but didn't comment.

"She's gonna pull through," he said, then took another sip of the amber liquid.

"Have you been able to see her?"

I knew he'd visited after me.

"Yeah. She didn't look as bad as I thought she would. Looked awfully pale, but still so beautiful and peaceful. Like some fairy tale princess. Jeez," he added, "listen to me."

I understood the feeling.

Q took a bite out of his burger, smiled, and closed his eyes, savoring the juicy moment.

"Have you thought anymore about who might possibly have any motivation to shoot her?"

He frowned and put the burger down. "Sure, I have. Thought about it a lot." He was looking off into the distance now, thinking about what he'd been thinking about.

I waited.

"As I said, you couldn't hardly dislike her. She's a beautiful soul. She doesn't hate nobody. Her feelings are all there, right on top for anyone to see and some to take advantage of. She hurts sometimes, but she don't take it out on people. But..." He took another puff on his cigarette, another sip of whiskey, another bite of his burger.

He took his time. I let him.

"...there's three people I can think of. I don't see any of them being the culprits, but somebody has to be, so I don't know what to think."

He paused, took a deep breath, let it out slowly, and said, "We got the boyfriends, Christopher and Speed Weed, and then there's—

"Speed Weed?" I asked.

Q chuckled, coughed, cleared his throat. "Yup. That's his name. Says he made it up himself because his West Virginia folks screwed up big time when they named him. I told him I couldn't imagine they did any worse than him, and he didn't think that was too funny. Anyway, he was her full-time manager and part-time boyfriend until about a year ago when Sarah decided he never was going to change for the better. She's a smart girl, but sometimes too forgiving. Speed, like a lot of his ilk, is a slippery son-of-a-gun, a fast talker, and a smooth operator. He was always full of promises about what he was going to do for her, but none of them ever came true, and he was taking too big a share out of her income. As a boyfriend, he was even worse. She found out he was sleeping with three or four of his other 'protégés,'" Q made quotation marks with his fingers, "as he called his female clientele."

"Was he angry when she dropped him?"

"Sure. She threw him out of her bed and her business at the same time. A double whammy. Most men would be hurting bad losing a woman like her. I hear maybe he's been hitting the candy pretty hard the last months."

"Cocaine?"

He nodded.

"Was he ever violent with her or threatening in any way?"

"Not that I saw or she ever said."

"Is he around at all? Have you seen him?"

"A few times over the past few months. He comes and goes. Looks for talent in the nightclubs. He's still in the business, still carrying on. He hasn't had any breakout talent, but I guess he does okay."

"I guess we have to learn more about him. Can you help there? Do you have contacts or sources in the music or nightclub business that might know more?"

Q pursed his lips, nodded. "Yeah. I been at this for a while. More'n forty years bumbling around the San Francisco scene with a couple of breaks when I went to New York to make my fortune. Loved New York. It didn't love me back. So I was already thinking about askin' around about my old friend Speed. I know a couple of his girlfriends and just about every agent and producer and nightclub owner in town. I'll see what they have to say."

"Good. I'll do some checking too, but it sounds like your sources might be a whole lot better than what I can do." I paused, sipped out of the straw to my malt and added, "How about Christopher?"

Before he could respond, I quickly summarized my visit to the Wambaugh residence.

"Doesn't surprise me," he said. "He's a spoilt boy. I don't think he's a bad kid, but he's too soft for life as we know it. I don't think he really loved Sarah. It was more a need. Like he'd lost something and was trying to replace it and latched on to Sarah for dear life." He took another toke of the cigarette and frowned at the table nearest us where four young men in sport coats and ties were quietly drinking red wine and playing Hearts. An unusually well-behaved group. I gathered that they had tickets for the Kronos Quartet that evening.

"Shit, I don't know, but he acted like a love-sick puppy, but I never bought it. Neither did Sarah, but I think she felt sorry for him. Soon as she met Rachel, things changed. I think that's the real thing. Nobody's fault, but it's gotta have upset little Christopher. I can't see him picking up a gun but..." His voice trailed off along with the smoke from his cigarette.

"So you never saw him show any signs of violence toward Sarah either?"

He shook his head.

"You said there was a third person that made you a little suspicious."

"Yeah." He had his whiskey glass at his mouth and tapped it against his lips, his eyes wandering into a dark corner of the room. "The old lady."

"Mrs. Wambaugh?"

He nodded. "I haven't met her, so I can't claim any real feeling there. But from what Sarah has said, she's one mean, ornery woman. Sarah couldn't figure it out. Didn't know if it was because of Christopher or Rachel or both of them. Anyway, the way I see it, she could have hired somebody. A hitman."

The four well-behaved young men had finished playing Hearts, and suddenly they stood up and began undressing. In moments, they had stripped down to matching red thongs and black tank tops. They whooped in unison.

From loudspeakers overhead a driving, thumping hip-hop beat filled the air.

The men charged off to a far corner of the room to a table of young half-drunk women. Pandemonium followed, with dancing men undulating their crotches suggestively at the shrieking, hysterical females.

"That's more like it," Q said. "Was wondering what those boys were up to."

"Bachelorette party," I mumbled.

"Guessin' so." Q shook his head. "Women have come a long way since my day."

"They certainly have," I agreed, watching the licentious display unfolding. The thongs barely contained their contents, and the women, glazed eyes wide with a combination of excitement and fear, reached out to fondle briefly, then shrieked some more.

It didn't look like fun to me. I've never been a fan of strip shows or gentlemen's clubs or any other public display of what should be private erotica. We men have ogled and used women as objects from time immemorial and look at the pathetic state it's gotten us to in male-female relationships.

I guess women should have the same right.

To sleep, perchance to dream—ay, there's the rub! For in that sleep of death, what dreams may come...must give us pause.

Shakespeare, I think, was trying to say, in his own inimitable way, that you have to be careful of what you want or desire because it might come packed with things you never expected.

I'm just saying.

The men were seated now, and several of the women had perched on their laps. Lips and hands and legs were fluttering, intertwined. I'd seen enough and turned back to Q. "Did you just dream up the part about Mrs. Wambaugh hiring somebody to kill Sarah, or do you actually know something."

Q's eyes twinkled. "Made the whole thing up. Got no basis for it."

I smiled and took another sip of my malt. "So, I think—"

"You ever seen that movie, *The Shining*?"

"Yes. Pretty unnerving."

"I seen it five or six times. Remember the black man, my man, Scatman Crothers? He could shine. He could see what the poor little white boy was suffering through. He could communicate with him through his mind and see things that happened in the past and maybe what was going to happen?"

The movie was unique and memorable, and I nodded, waiting for him to make his point.

Q breathed in through his nose and then let it go. "I'm not

saying I can shine, not like in the movie. But my mother always said I had a gift. I could sense when something bad was going to happen and eight times out of ten I was right. I can't communicate with somebody else through my mind, but sometimes I get a humming, a weird feeling in my mind about somebody. In this case, I got it when Sarah was talking about the old lady."

"I'm not doubting your feelings, Q, but we need more than—"

"Not saying that she had somebody try and kill Sarah. Just that I wouldn't at all be surprised if she did. You get that?"

I got it, and I had to admit that I agreed with him. It wouldn't much shock me either if Mrs. Wambaugh turned out to be behind the shooting although it was more than a little puzzling that she would have dragged me into the situation right before she did so.

People are strange and that ain't the half of it.

THIRTEEN

I couldn't remember the last time I'd been to the Japanese tea gardens in Golden Gate Park. My mom used to take me there when I was a kid. She'd have her tea, and I'd munch on fortune cookies and give greater significance than deserved to the simple, clichéd messages on the slips of paper nestled inside them.

In my twenties, I did remember bringing a college girlfriend here who was from Wauwatosa, Wisconsin. She loved the park, the gardens, the tea, and me.

I used to rib her about her home town. Calling it Wow Wow Tosa.

She called me a coastal elitist and found me, at one and the same time, amusing and annoying.

I can't say it's the first time I've been met with those mixed feelings.

Our love blossomed for a while, but then withered, as love is wont to do.

Last I heard, she'd moved back to her hometown and was working in marketing at the Pabst Milwaukee Brewery there.

Wow Wow.

Rachel sat at the irori, the farmhouse-style family table, across from me.

I'd asked to meet with her at her apartment in the Embarcadero, but she'd said that she'd rather meet somewhere else. As the result of my chat with Phoebe, the first thing that popped into my mind was the tea gardens.

The five-acre gardens are a cornucopia of Japanese beauty—pagodas and stone lanterns and a koi pond topped by an arched drum bridge served by stepping stone paths and lots of cherry blossom trees that bloomed in March and April.

I ordered Hojicha, a tea roasted over charcoal that gives it a smoky flavor, along with some miso soup. Rachel had iced green tea and edamame.

After we received our tea, Rachel said, "Such a coincidence. Sarah loves it here. We came here quite a few times."

I didn't bother mentioning that it was less of a coincidence than it seemed.

"So, Mr. Plank—"

"Max, please."

"Max, I'm happy to meet with you, but I don't know what else I can tell you that I haven't already told the detectives."

"You'd be surprised. It's been a couple of days. Sometimes, after a traumatic event like this one, even though you weren't there, our unconscious mind starts making connections. And, even if there's nothing new, I wanted you to tell me what you told the police. Sometimes fresh ears are all that's needed to sift out overlooked details or clues."

She nodded as if that made sense. I'd been ad-libbing, not to say bullshitting, so I was glad to see I hadn't totally confused her.

"So you just want me to tell you what I told the detectives about me and Sarah and where I was that day and anything that

Sarah may have said about anyone that might be a threat to her and—"

"All of that, yes. Let's start there." I gave her a reassuring smile and nodded.

"Well, first of all, I was...jeez, I am...we're...together. Sarah and me."

"You're dating?"

"More than that."

"That must be awkward."

She raised her eyebrows and started to protest. "You don't approve of same-sex—"

"No. No. I don't care what any two people to or for each other in the privacy of their own homes." I didn't add that some of my best friends are gay. While true, I felt it would cheapen my argument. "I mean your brother...didn't he just break up with Sarah? Wasn't he in love with her?"

Sarah looked away, glanced down, noticed her tea cup, the steam rising like a little smoke signal. She picked it up. Blew on the pooling liquid. Put it back down. Stared into it. There were leaves at the bottom of the cup, so maybe she was trying to read them.

"Sarah's relationship with my brother wasn't mutual. He...kind of became a little obsessed after seeing her perform. He approached her after a show. He can be charming, at times, but he's pretty awkward around women. She did like him at first, they went out on and off for a couple of months, but it was very one-sided overall."

"Why was your mother so alarmed about the relationship?"

She gave me a quizzical look.

"Your mother hired me to investigate Sarah. That's why I was there that night."

"You're kidding?"

I was surprised. She'd lived with her mother for more than

twenty years. I'd only spent a couple of hours with the woman and by now wouldn't be shocked if she asked me to kill Sarah.

"I kid you not."

She shook her head and wrinkled her nose. "Mother can be such a pain in the ass."

"I talked with Christopher yesterday, before your mother threw me off the property, and he still seemed pretty upset by the breakup."

"You were at the house?"

I shrugged.

"Uninvited?"

I shrugged again.

She laughed. "You're a brave one."

"Some might call it foolhardy."

"For sure. My mother is a powerful person. She knows lots of influential people. You'd better be careful."

"I speak truth to power," I said with a smile.

She gave me a quizzical look and shook her head. "You're kind of a smart ass."

"Flattery will get you nowhere," I quipped.

She rolled her eyes at me.

"How did you and Sarah meet?"

"Christopher took me to see her sing and, well, she was just so wonderful." She glanced up at me and said, "You know. You've seen her."

"She's extraordinary."

Rachel nodded her head up and down. "Absolutely. Anyway, afterward, the three of us went out to eat, and then I'd see her now and then when Christopher brought her home." She blushed, wrapped her hands around her tea cup. "There was always something going on between us. Chemistry, to use a cliché, was there from the first time I laid eyes on her. I know she felt it, too. Once it was obvious her and Christopher were finished, she called me…"

"Tell me about recent days. Anything unusual that might relate to the shooting?"

She summarized what she'd told the police, and there was nothing, at least on the surface of it, that seemed particularly notable. Sarah hadn't been upset or fearful or anguished in any way. She was a little sad about Christopher, but knew that it was best to break it off sooner rather than later, as she had no romantic feelings for him. Rachel wasn't aware of any new people in Sarah's life or anything that would signal trouble.

When she finished, I thanked her and then asked, "Tell me about your father."

Her mouth closed. She started nibbling on her lower lip with her upper teeth.

"I'm sorry, Max, but I don't…see how he has anything to do with any of this."

I didn't either, but the more people refused to tell me anything about dear old dad, the more interesting he became to me.

"Listen, Rachel, crimes, cases like this, sometimes seem to have no rhyme or reason. But they always do. There's always an underlying pulse, and a genesis, perhaps a distant one. As I said, your mother hired me. That alone is a little strange, coming as it did so close to Sarah's shooting. I was only there to witness it because of your mom. And my sources tell me there's a big mystery surrounding your dad. He seems to be a ghost, although he's still alive. He may have nothing to do with current events, but my job is to tug on every loose string to pull on each loose tangent, no matter how removed it appears. The police will likely get to your dad, but this isn't the only case they have, and it might take some time."

She sighed, touched her forehead, and grimaced as if her head hurt. "My dad left us when we were in our teens. I haven't seen him in almost nine years. My mother won't speak about him. We're not even allowed to mention his name in front of her."

"He is still alive?"

"Yes. I'm sure he is. I don't know…Mom had him working at the company. Maybe he still does. But he didn't do much. It was mainly ceremonial, from what I can gather. He lived off her money. To be blunt, he's a narcissist. A sick man."

"But you have no idea where he is?" I wanted to know a lot more about the nature of his sickness.

She paused, bit her lip again, grimaced. "Just rumors. I've heard Mother talking on the phone. When this or that executive or financial person visits the house, I've overheard things."

"And…" I said, drawing the word out.

"And…he may be in Las Vegas. The family has interests there. A casino and other properties. The rumor is that he lives there in one of the properties, but I don't know anything else."

"And he's had no contact with you or Christopher. No letters or emails or cards at Christmas?"

She shook her head, a wounded faraway look in her eyes.

"Do you know if your mother has had contact?"

"I think so. She must. But she refuses to say a word about it."

"Do you know why he left?"

Another long, pointed pause before she said, "He was difficult. My parents' relationship was never good. Although she was crazy about him. I never could understand it." She paused, reflecting. "He has his charms. And he's very good looking. But he isn't a nice man. He can be very mean. To his wife and to his children. I'm sorry, but I don't want to talk about him anymore."

I wanted to press, but I saw the pain in her eyes, and decided to pursue dear old dad using other avenues.

I handed her a fortune cookie and told her to read it to me.

She visibly relaxed, snapped the cookie open, and read, "A new voyage will fill your life with untold memories."

She smiled and told me to read mine.

I cracked it open and read it to myself. *Be on the lookout for coming events; they cast their shadows beforehand.*

"Read it to me, Max."

I said, "It never pays to kick a skunk," and added, "or massage a porcupine."

She laughed, while I thought about the real message in the cookie I'd gotten and wondered if the universe was trying to tell me something.

FOURTEEN

While I'd been sharing tea and cookies with Rachel, Marsh had been breaking into Sarah's little cottage. We were sitting on a bench near Stow Lake in the middle of Golden Gate Park. It was a cool, overcast day, the sun shunted behind gray clouds. The grass surrounding us glistened wetly from the morning fog. It had been recently cut and smelled pleasantly pungent.

Nearby, runners ran, bicyclists bicycled, lovers loved or, at least kissed, readers read, frisbee throwers frisbeed.

We surveyed this varied scene and, after I gave him the highlight of my chat with Rachel, Marsh brought me up to date on how he'd been spending his time.

He'd been a busy boy and there was lots to tell.

Proceeding in reverse chronological order, he told me what he'd found inside Sarah's small cottage. I didn't ask him how he'd manage to bridge her fortifications as most people's houses are a breeze for anyone with a modicum of skill. The primary danger is nosy neighbors, but Marsh has phantom-like qualities.

"Quite a cozy abode," he said, his eyes following the high arc of a blue frisbee. "She's got taste in music and furnishings. Good jazz collection with the proper classical dose. Nice Victorian decor without getting too cutesy. Just the right amount of edge. Not a lot of money, but she spends it well. She's a neatnik, too. I think we'd schmooze well."

"Good to know. Soon as she wakes up, I'll give her your number."

"Setting the scene, dear boy." A runner passed us by wearing thongish red shorts. "If you're going to show it off, it helps having an ass like his," Marsh commented admiringly, continuing, "The neatness extends to her files, both off and online. Good systems. Well-labeled folders. It wasn't hard to sift through the ins and outs of her life of late."

"So you didn't have any password problems?"

"Actually, she was better than most in her creativity. But I had Portia at the ready, and she opened up everything remotely for me within minutes."

It didn't surprise me. Portia had helped me on several cases. She had elite hacking skills.

"Any whew, our subject's finances could be better. She's got a little savings, and I do mean little. No investments. Enough money to last her for maybe three months. Current income barely covers modest expenses."

"You should hear her sing. She should be rolling in dough."

"She sings jazz. We live amongst philistines."

Twenty yards from us, a couple laying on a blue blanket untangled and stopped kissing. The curly-haired blonde coed sat up, brushed something off her prominent breasts, and cursed. The boy beneath her put his hands behind his head and said, "C'mon, Chrissie. I didn't mean anything by it."

"Screw you," she said.

"I was hoping," he joked.

But it was the wrong thing to say. She slapped his face and jumped to her feet. The boy looked stunned.

"I'm tired of it, Rob."

"Chrissie—" He lifted a hand, reaching out to her. "Okay. Sit back down. People are watching. I didn't mean it anyway. Let's not do this again."

She put her hands on her hips and stared off into the distance, ignoring him.

"Chrissie," he implored, wriggling his fingers in a come-hither gesture.

"I'm going home."

"Okay. Let's go home."

"To Charlotte, Rob."

"What are you talking about?"

She turned and left him there, walking purposefully into her future.

"Chrissie," he whined. "Chrissie?" he asked, confused, bothered, and bewildered.

"He's lost her," Marsh said.

"He knows it, too."

"Besides her precarious financial condition, Ms. Swan has had three relationships of note in the past year. I didn't have access to her phone. I assume the police confiscated that at the scene of the crime."

I assumed the same, but they weren't sharing their info with me.

"They probably haven't gotten a warrant to search her apartment yet. I imagine they're waiting to interview her first. It appears that Sarah had a romantic connection with both young Christopher and his sister. Quite the sticky wicket."

"Yes, that's what I thought. Rachel admitted as much to me today."

"Doesn't that ring all sorts of alarm bells?"

"Yes and no," I said. "It could be the key to the shooting. Or just love's arrow having no truck with reason or logic or family ties."

"I lean toward the former explanation."

"Of course you do. You're a control freak. You don't let love sway you."

"Love, or rather, lust, wreaks havoc on those who allow it to. I keep my lust leashed to my higher purposes."

I've never seen Marsh go gaga over any lover. I don't think he's ever been deeply in love. He loves sex and has it regularly. He doesn't exactly use people, but he seems always to be firmly in control of his feelings and urges.

That's been a problem with Tom, his current and longest-lasting relationship, going on almost two years. Tom wants love and marriage. Both words are anathema to Marsh.

"Did you see any messages to or from Christopher or Rachel that indicated trouble?"

"Yes. But not the I'm-going-to-murder-you kind. She'd stopped responding to Christopher's pleadings. He was emailing and messaging her through Facebook several times a day for a couple of weeks and she'd asked him to stop. He didn't and so she ignored him. In the couple of weeks before the shooting, the messages had dwindled to a few. Quite pathetic. And whiney. She was much too patient with him. I had to keep reading to make sure there was nothing there, but they made my stomach turn. I wanted to take him by the lapels and shake him and tell him to man up."

"But he never threatened her or said anything that might have indicated real craziness?"

"No. Just weakness."

"How about Rachel?"

"Kind of the opposite of her little brother. The first messages started roughly three months ago when Sarah was first trying to break off with Christopher. In the past months, the messages on both ends got more affectionate. They signed off using the L word. No strong indication that they were having sex, although I'd bet a pretty penny they are, but, of course, they're female so not quite so crude and rude as the weaker sex."

"Anything else?"

He looked over at Rob, who was sitting on his blue blanket looking like he'd just lost his girlfriend. "She had a manager of some kind. Looks like she fired him about a year ago. It appears they were lovers, too. It appears to have been messy. Speed was angry with her when she cut him off, personally and professionally."

"Yes, Q told me a bit about him, and he's going to follow up with his contacts in the music business to see if he can find out more about his recent doings. Any threatening messages from him?"

"Not in the past several months. He did say he was going to sue her. I'll look into that and him."

"Okay. Anything else?"

"There were four zip drives that I found in a desk drawer. I haven't looked at them yet, as I didn't want to linger in the apartment too long. I assume that they're mostly backup for her hard drive, but I'll have a look at them soon to confirm."

"Okay. Anything else."

"She is hot. Saw photos."

"Do you ever feel any kind of moral qualms or ickiness about invading someone's privacy like this, because I do."

"None whatsoever. Better me than others. I'm reliable and trustworthy. Her secrets are safe with me."

"I'm sure she'd be comforted by that."

He shrugged. "So where are we at here?"

I sighed. "I don't know. Christopher has to be our top suspect at this point. The only thing is I don't see him as capable of it. He's immature and soft. He might have gotten carried away, rushed to the club, and shot her in the spur of a rash moment, but I think there was a little more method to the madness. First of all, you're right, the fact that I was there is too coincidental. Someone likely wanted me there or wanted to get rid of her before I talked to her. Secondly, the flowers and the break-a-leg message. Innocent on the surface but also suspicious as hell. And why twenty roses? Of course, that means the shooter was tipping his or her hand, like they weren't too worried about being caught, but also needed to convey their dislike of Sarah overtly before trying to kill her."

"Who else?"

"Mrs. Wambaugh. She really hated and was threatened by Sarah. This old boyfriend/manager Speed just because of the animosity you describe. The father, Fogerty you said his name was, because he's so mysterious… Any word on him, by the way?"

"Nothing yet. He seems to have covered his tracks pretty well. I have people working on it though. I imagine we'll have something soon."

"I told you he's probably in Las Vegas."

Marsh nodded. "How about her bandmates? Phoebe? The old guitar player?"

"They both love her. I see nothing but sincerity and genuine affection there."

"Can't eliminate them yet."

I knew he was right, but I'd already done so.

"Next steps?"

"You keep after Mr. Wambaugh, and do you think you can have someone follow Christopher for a couple of days? I'd like to know where he goes, what he does. Hopefully, he leaves the house every now and then."

"Sure."

"And I'm going to take another crack at Mrs. Wambaugh."

"You're a glutton for punishment."

Sometimes it did seem I had masochistic tendencies.

FIFTEEN

Bo Fiddler is my oldest friend. We were in a band together throughout college and into our twenties. We were a local semi-sensation and got a little radio play for a few of our songs. We probably came as close to making it as most good bands.

But, ultimately, time and friction with various members of our band, to say nothing of drugs and alcohol, took their toll.

None of it ever came between Bo and me.

I was in the kitchen of the Rusty Root, Bo's restaurant at Fisherman's Wharf. Rope Rivers, his edgy, fabulous twenty-seven-year-old chef, was stirring a pot of cioppino. The seafood and tomato smells made my nose swoon and my mouth water.

Rope was wearing his ubiquitous bandana over his flaming red hair. His rosy cheeks were copiously freckled. He was the thinnest chef I'd ever seen. He dipped a large spoon into the soup and tasted, "Ahhh. Perfection."

"Max," he said and moved the spoon in front of my mouth. I sipped the broth. "Rope, you slay me."

He smiled, tapped my arm companionably, and turned back to his work.

Bo leaned back against one of the massive stainless-steel refrigerators, his arms folded across his chest, telling me about the troubles in his daughter's marriage.

"It's not a big surprise, Bo. They're too young to play house." I was Jen's Uncle Max, I loved her, but she was only nineteen. Her betrothed was the same age. They'd been married less than a year.

"Doesn't make it any easier. They don't have any money. He keeps getting fired from his minimum wage jobs. She was going to be a veterinarian but now she's working as a waitress in a diner. She doesn't tell me much, but I can see it on her face. My happy-go-lucky baby girl is feeling the weight of the world. I've offered to pay for her to go back to college, but she won't take the money."

"That's a good sign."

"It's stupid. Unless Brad locates a little gumption or ambition, they're heading nowhere fast."

"They're young. They can still work it out."

"I guess. But I can't tell if he's treating her right. She hasn't said anything, but before they were married, she couldn't stop gushing about him. Now she just says they're doing fine. Never tells me how wonderful he is. He'd better be, or I'm going to break..." Bo paused and them mumbled, "Shit."

It was early afternoon, so the kitchen wasn't bustling yet. Rope and the sous chef were the only other people nearby.

"Lookit, if you find out he's not treating her right, that's one thing. But there's no reason to go there right now. Most young couples struggle in a lot of ways early on. She wants to make her own way. She's a sensible girl, at least outside of her decision to marry Brad. Trust her."

"That's what Sandra says, too. I'm probably overreacting."

I knew he wasn't going to stop worrying. I'd been worrying

since I'd first heard about the wedding plans. No one should get married before the age of thirty, and if they know what's good for them, they should wait until they're forty or, better yet, forget the whole damn thing.

Turning to the real reason I'd come to the Rusty Root, I said, "Bo, I need a favor."

"What else is new?" he quipped. "Hit me."

"I want you and Rope to throw a dinner for me."

"What are we honoring you for?"

"It's not actually for me. It's for a very, very rich woman. It'll be at her house in Atherton. It'll be good publicity for you, and you'll have the opportunity to impress a lot of rich people."

"Is this woman going to pay for the event?"

"No. You're going to offer it to her for free. Turns out she's big fan of Rope's and is going to be thrilled."

"So I'm just going to donate the thousands of dollars it's going to cost?"

"That would be nice."

"But I'm not that nice a guy."

"I knew that. We'll pay for it."

Or, rather, Marsh would front the money and, eventually, I hoped that Mrs. Wambaugh would pay for it herself.

"That might work."

"But time is of the essence."

"When?" he asked, raising a suspicious eyebrow.

"This weekend."

"No way. Not possible. You're nuts."

I answered all three of his negative statements, and then we bickered for another ten minutes before he agreed to my terms.

SIXTEEN

I was on *Acapella Blues*, getting ready for a very exciting evening, making sure I had the right balance of tools for the task, when my cell phone rang.

Phoebe was on the line and said, excitedly, "I found it."

"What?"

"The note. With the flowers. I mean, I didn't find the flowers, but I found the note."

"Great. Can you read it to me?"

"It says just what I told you. It's typed so no way to identify from handwriting. It's addressed, *Dear Sarah. Break a Leg. Your ardent admirer.*"

"That's it?"

"Sorry."

"It's okay. It's great you found it. Where are you now?"

"At the club. I'll be here for another couple of hours."

"I'm going to send someone over to pick it up."

"You going to try and trace it somehow?"

"I'll probably turn it over to the police and have them look for fingerprints or any other traces that might help. Thanks again," I said.

I was expecting a five p.m. call from Marsh, and it came in on the button as I was drinking an espresso and munching on a vanilla biscotti out on my deck. There was a middling breeze ruffling my hair and my cool black shirt, but the sky was mostly blue, and the sun was heading south and west when I said, "Marsh," into my cell phone.

"I'm at the *Sweet and Sour*. Everything's set."

"How's Dao?"

"Basket case."

"I don't blame him." Even though Meiying was at Alexandra's place with Frankie and out of harm's way, this had to be unnerving for my good friend.

"Takeshi's gang is supposed to arrive at eleven. I'm going to catch a bite with Tom and get back here by nine. You should do the same."

I hung up the phone and called Frankie.

She answered on the first ring and said, "Max. I miss you."

"Me too," I said. "I'll take you to a movie tomorrow. Okay?"

"Okay."

"Can I speak to Meiying?"

"She's making meatballs and spaghetti."

"Great. I just need her for a minute."

Frankie disappeared, and a few seconds later, Meiying said, "Plank."

"How's everything there?"

"Very well. We are having good time. Frankie is making me make spaghetti. For her, I do it. How's Dao?"

"He's okay. A little nervous, of course. Marsh is with him, and I'm going over. We'll take good care of him and get rid of those bad boys."

"I trust you. But if anything happen to my Dao…" She paused. I could hear her breathing softly on the other end of the line.

"Nothing will happen to him. I promise."

As those words came out of my mouth, I understood that sometimes we just say things to people we care about to try and make them and ourselves feel better.

SEVENTEEN

The supply room connected to the bar was as neat and orderly as you'd expect from Dao and Meiying. One wall had a floor to ceiling cabinet filled with dining and party accoutrements: plates, cups, glasses, napkins, bowls, and utensils appropriate to various party motifs. A wine rack with about a hundred bottles sat beside a boxful of hard liquor bottles and a giant stainless-steel refrigerator. Beside it, a sharp wall indentation held cleaning supplies, mops, and brooms. The room had a red and white checkerboard linoleum floor and a ceiling painted light blue. It smelled of lemon polish with a floral accent.

I stood leaning against the door jamb trying to keep Dao's spirits up. He sat at the bar nursing a green tea and fidgeting nervously with a nautical map of San Francisco Bay. All of us, save perhaps Marsh, would rather be sailing away than facing the remains of this day.

Marsh was enjoying a whiskey sour from an adjacent bedroom connected to the sky lounge and bar by a short corridor not visible from the main part of the room.

We'd debated confronting them openly, all three of us, but

decided to let the Yakuza wannabes get comfortable with their big advantage before surprising them with the fact that things might be a little more complicated than they'd hoped for.

We also thought it might be best to observe them as they circled their prey and thus gauge their level of sophistication, malevolence, and intent with Dao, before letting them know that the game had changed, that the demon would have to slay a dragon and not just an aging financial wizard to earn his payday.

It was seven minutes after eleven p.m. when I heard steps out on the gangplank.

I moved back into the supply room and tipped the door until I had narrow sliver of sight into the bar area.

Dao spun his stool toward the door to the sky lounge and clutched his knees with his hands.

It took more than just a few minutes for the young men to enter the room. I heard footsteps traveling up and down the gangway and onto the boat. Noise above and below me. They were obviously casing the joint, trying to make sure that Dao had complied with their demands and was facing them alone.

Marsh had stationed one of his men in an inconspicuous hangout near the dock most of the day, keeping an eye out for the comings and goings in and around the *Sweet and Sour*, and he'd reported back that there'd been no sign of anyone else doing the same.

Finally, they entered the sky lounge. Dao fixed his eyes on something at the far end of the room.

"Old man, you've been a bad boy, haven't you?" a chiding, high-pitched voice said.

Dao glanced toward me and then quickly glanced away.

"Your friends can't save you, old man."

So they had been watching. I wondered briefly if it was from a nearby building or boat that Marsh's man might have missed.

Steps above me. Steps below me. They weren't casing the joint.

Takeshi had brought a large contingent, and they knew where we were and were surrounding us hoping to engineer their own little Custer's Last Stand.

I watched Dao through my slender porthole, and he didn't look good. His face was drained of color.

"Old man, tell your friends to show themselves. We know they are in this room. Tell Max Plank that we know where he is hiding Meiying. Tell him the Demon lurks close to her and the little girl."

I felt like somebody had just punched me in the gut. I opened the door and stepped out into the bar, behind Dao.

"Hello, Max Plank."

Takeshi was a handsome brute with a small nose, high cheekbones, and unusual light brown eyes. He was thin but looked in shape. Beneath an expensive-looking black sport coat, he wore a long-sleeved black shirt and black jeans. He smiled at me when he said my name. He was happy to see me, which almost, but not quite, made my day.

Behind Takeshi stood a half-dozen young Chinese males. All possessed a certain *élan*, a dangerous *je ne sais quoi*. Four held pistols with silencers, two held Uzis, their barrels pointed sideways, away from us.

More noise from the deck above ours.

"Where is your friend, Max Plank?"

"He's hard to keep track of. Don't know where he's gone to at the moment."

"Max Plank, don't play games. This is serious business." And still, he was smiling.

"I am not my brother's keeper, Takeshi."

While we bantered and I studied the whole gang gathered so aggressively in front of me, I remembered the briefing that Marsh had given me earlier in the day. He'd discovered that George Liu's nature was not dissimilar to Dao's. He'd started buying houses and apartments in Hong Kong and ended up owning shopping centers in America. In middle age, he'd parlayed his real estate holdings into an import-export business and had prospered further. Everything he'd ever touched had turned to gold, or at least tarnished silver. He was now in his eighties, a widower, living with his extended family in Santa Rosa. No hints of corruption or overt criminal activity, although that doesn't mean there weren't any.

His younger brother, Ling, a modest man by all appearances, followed his brother to the new world and ended up working at the Santa Rosa post office where he labored for forty years until his recent retirement.

Ling's son, Takeshi, appeared to be rather unimpressed by his father's modest achievements and wanted a faster route to the top than his successful uncle's. He'd been arrested for petty theft when he was thirteen. Assault and battery when he was fifteen and armed robbery when he was seventeen. He'd spent a fair amount of time at juvenile halls but had somehow avoided real prison so far. Maybe George Liu had saved him with expensive lawyers.

He had no arrests for the past five years, which made him either lucky or smart.

In the light of this evening, I guessed he was both.

"We cannot discuss business until your friend is with us. Do you want my boys to search for him? It might end in significant damage to this vessel."

His syntax belied his involvement with the juvenile justice system, and I guessed he was something of an autodidact.

Something or, rather, someone, crashed to the burnished teak flooring of the deck above us. A muffled thud, a grunt, another loud floor slam.

Takeshi's eyes rolled upward and studied the ceiling. I didn't bother.

Another thud, something large, like a human being, hitting the floor followed by something smaller, like a book slammed on a table. I guessed it was the sound of a gun with a suppressor going off.

Takeshi looked back at me, alarmed and confused for a moment.

"I believe my friend has been found by your boys. Or, rather, vice versa, unfortunately. For them, I mean."

Despite my outer calm, large ungainly butterflies bumped into each other in my chest.

The typical flight-or-fight response.

I do have the ability to achieve a stillness, a focus inside, but it usually only happens at the very moment before danger or in the midst of an altercation.

It didn't used to be that way. Meditation, yoga, Marsh's tutoring, and, most importantly, an unseemly number of experiences fending off threatening behavior and actual violence have allowed me and my body and mind to jump into "lizard brain" mode when necessary.

Not always, but often. And it has saved my life more than once.

For Marsh, there seems to be no transition needed. He is always ready, and I've rarely seen him rattled by even the most extreme threats.

It's a gift, but not one that I envy.

I love Marsh, but I don't want his nature. I just want to learn enough to survive what I have to survive and avoid violence whenever possible.

Although there are people, some very close to me, that feel that I court it. I don't think I do, but it's part and parcel of what I do for a living.

Takeshi, his eyes wide, looked up again and shouted, "Charles!"

No response.

"John?"

Nada.

"Daniel?"

Daniel did not respond to the great leader.

"Baby!"

I guessed Baby was curled up in a fetal position.

Takeshi pulled a revolver from inside his coat and pointed it at Dao. "Call for him to surrender himself here or I will shoot the old man."

Before I could answer, Marsh appeared out of the hallway connected to the adjoining bedroom. He held the remains of the whiskey sour in his right hand but appeared otherwise weaponless.

Takeshi and all the others in the room sighted their guns on him. "Stay right where you are."

Since he didn't identify him by name, I assumed he didn't know who Marsh was.

Mistake numero uno.

Marsh flashed a smile and started moving toward the bar.

"Where are you going…" The gun waved up and down in Takeshi's hand.

He reached the bar, placed the empty glass on top of it, put his hand on top of Dao's shoulder. Something passed between them, and Dao got up and joined Marsh behind the bar.

"Stop! Stay where you are!"

Too late. Marsh and Dao achieved stasis behind the bar.

All guns and wide eyes in the room were trained on their every movement.

Takeshi shouted, "George! Ba! Come now!"

He glanced down at the floor, and I assumed those were the men I'd heard moving around beneath us earlier.

"'Fraid they're fast asleep, just like the others upstairs."

"You killed them?" Takeshi's voice reflected disbelief and alarm and reluctant admiration all at once.

"No. Fortunately, they were all quite cooperative. Some might call them sloppy or amateurish. But it saved their lives. I can't speak to the possibility of concussions."

"Who are you?" Takeshi asked, a sense of fear and uncertainty and the first gnarly touch of fear in his voice.

"Just a regular guy trying to keep his nose clean in a world inhabited by cretins like you and your associates."

"I would be careful, Mister…?"

"My friends call me Marsh. But you can call me Doctor Demento."

Takeshi did not know how to react. He looked at me, a little slack-jawed, his eyes wide, if not in panic, at least a rising level of confusion.

I shrugged. I empathized with him. Encountering Marsh doing what he does best for the first time can be profoundly mind boggling.

"So, Takeshi, you're here to negotiate. Why don't you explain your position? I only have it second-hand, and to be honest, I don't really believe, as honest as Dao is, that he's relayed your demand accurately. Because, man, it's really far out," I said, keeping my voice as steady as I could considering my racing heart and wobbly knees.

Takeshi muttered something in Chinese, and the men behind him moved forward a step. All of them racked the slides on their single-action semi-automatics.

He waved at his gang and their overwhelming weaponry. "You understand?" he said.

I nodded. Dao trembled. Marsh didn't do a thing.

"The old man cheated my uncle out of millions of dollars. Most of his savings. We expect justice. That is all. As an act of good faith, we have requested a small deposit. Did you bring it, old man?"

He glared at Dao, who looked away and stayed silent.

"That is disappointing, old man."

Young punk was getting on my nerves. If he called my friend old man one more time, I didn't know if I was going to be able to stop myself from making him eat his gun.

"It was just a small gesture of good will. The old man has the money and will still have enough left over to last him the rest of his days. This is the only way my family will feel avenged for this profound injustice. It is fortunate that we do not believe in violence for violence's sake, since, had this treachery been committed back in our ancestral home, the old man would have forfeited his life."

"Sounds fair," Marsh purred like a big cat. "Are you sure you don't want to ask for more? Perhaps Plank or I can kick in some money for having inconvenienced you tonight? Do you have taxi fare home?"

"This isn't a laughing matter," Takeshi growled.

"Only your demands are joke-worthy. If your uncle really gambled that much money on a speculative risk like this one, then something is wrong with him and the family should take him to a doctor. In any case, he was given all the proper warnings, but he chose to ignore them. Our friend Dao here has no responsibility and will not pay you a single solitary nickel. You continue to threaten him at great peril to your health and well-being. I suggest you leave right now while you still can."

Takeshi's look morphed from astonishment to grim smugness. "You may have surprised my men upstairs in the dark. But it is not dark now. And…" he glanced at me, "I have someone outside of your girlfriend's house with Meiying and the little girl." He reached into his pocket and removed his cell phone and waved it. "One phone call and they both disappear."

"So you're going to kill us?" Marsh asked. "You think you'll slaughter us and skip out of here scot-free, assuming we haven't already told the police all about your little gang?"

Takeshi smiled. "Makes no matter. You'll be dead, and what happens to us is none of your concern."

"That's a relief," Marsh said.

"So," Takeshi said, looking to Dao, "will you provide this small gesture of good faith?"

Dao opened his mouth to answer, but Marsh touched his arm and said flatly, "Not one plum nickel."

Takeshi shook his head and started punching buttons on his phone. He stood watching us and listening for a long time. The rings were audible in the deathly quiet of the room. Ten rings. Fifteen. Twenty. With each passing peal, the confidence on his face cratered just a little. Finally, he clicked his phone off, swore, and said, "Ban will call back soon."

"I doubt it," Marsh said. "I paid a visit to Meiying just before I arrived here. Ban is all tied up at the moment."

"Fuck you," he screamed, lifting and leveling his piece.

Marsh's hands rose from beneath the bar. When they appeared above the beautiful walnut veneer, each gripped a hand grenade.

With his thumbs, he jerked the pins free. They hit the floor with dual pings.

Takeshi jumped back, his gun flagging.

Marsh and Dao dove beneath the bar. Dao's face was white as a ghost. I couldn't see Marsh, just his hands primed to throw hanging fast balls.

"Now, gentlemen, I suggest you file out in an orderly manner. The bar will protect us from the force of the explosions, but I fear all of you might lose limb and life," Marsh said calmly from his crouched position.

Feeling left out, I dived behind the cover of the bar. "'Bout time, buddy," Marsh said.

"You're crazy, man," Takeshi screamed. "The old man will pay."

He barked commands in Chinese to his compatriots. Chatter ensued. Then, slowly, I heard the shuffling of shoes. I inched around to the edge of the bar and peeked out in time to see them disappearing out the door. More steps on the stairs rising to the upper deck. Scuffling, groans, whispers, heavy lifting as they retrieved their wounded from above and below.

Then I heard the whole bunch of them stumble and bumble their way down the gangplank and onto the pier and away from the *Sweet and Sour*.

Marsh stood up and put the grenades on top of the bar. Most people, including myself before being educated by Marsh, are misled by the movies. They think that the pin being released on a hand grenade means it will explode within seconds. Not true. The trigger, the long handle on the side of the bomb, is the actual detonator. Once the grenade is thrown, the trigger gets loose, the fuse is engaged, and three or four seconds later...boom!

Still, I looked at the grenades with more than a little wariness, and said, "Marsh," nodding toward the bombs.

He winked at me, searched the floor, found the pins, and reinserted them.

I took a deep breath. It felt like the first I had taken in a month.

EIGHTEEN

The shimmery, bronze-toned curtain dropped with a shallow whoosh and billowed like a sail in a stiff headwind before settling lightly on the gleaming bamboo floor.

I had no idea what I had just seen meant, but it had a seductive quality to it, a compelling otherworldly feel.

"We're going to have English narration. Headphones."

"That will be helpful."

"I wasn't in favor of it. I'm an originalist, so to speak. I think the movements, the pageantry, the costumes convey all you need. But Dao insisted. He has less faith in us."

"Surprising." I've never known Marsh to be overly optimistic about humans, especially of the American variety.

We were sitting on unpainted makeshift benches in the center of the still-developing theater complex near the Aquarium on Fisherman's Wharf.

"What did you think?"

Marsh had just finished explaining a bit about Kabuki—how it had been invented in Japan by a woman and performed for common people exclusively by women in the early sixteenth century. Within thirty years, the patriarchal powers that be were threatened by the erotic nature of the spectacle and banned women from participating. Since then it has been an exclusively male art, with men playing female roles. Kabuki—meaning sing, dance, and skill in Japanese—is highly stylized with elaborate costumes, makeup, outrageous wigs, and over-the-top acting. It's basically a bombastic dance-theater spectacle. I felt it had more than a few similarities to opera.

The gorgeous curtain I had just seen fall was just one aspect of the dynamic staging. Marsh said they were designing trap doors and revolving platforms and overhead wiring that would allow the actors to take flight above the audience.

Kimonos would be offered to all patrons to get them into the proper mood.

"I don't know what was going on, but it felt like I was in another world. Strange and wonderful."

"That's the idea."

A man wearing a horrific mask—a Joker-esque mouth with demon orange eyes and black horns—walked toward us.

"Haruki, it was beautiful. Bravo."

The man slipped off the mask. He was a slender, boyish-looking man in his forties with expressive eyes and jet-black hair.

"Thank you, Mr. Chapin. Did you like the oyama?" Haruki looked apprehensive.

"Yes, tell Ichiro it was good."

Haruki's smile broadened, he gave a little bow, to which Marsh responded with a nod, and disappeared behind the curtain.

"Oyama?"

"The female role, played by a male, of course. Ichiro just signed on. Haruki recruited him from Kyoto. That's where I found Haruki, who is, more or less, our director and lead actor."

I didn't know how Marsh could differentiate between what

was good and bad acting, as most of the faces were covered in elaborate makeup or garish masks, and all the performances were extravagant to the extreme, but, as I say, it all wove a spell that was fascinating.

"When does the theater open?"

"Not until next summer. Lots still to do, the theater itself is months from completion. Green tea," he said and got up.

I followed him to a small anteroom in back of the theater where a pot of hot green tea sat on a Formica table. The tea cups were decorated with Kabuki masks, as was the pot. Marsh sat and poured the tea. I took the seat across from him.

"How's Dao doing?" I asked, knowing Marsh had dropped by the *Sweet and Sour* earlier that morning.

"Shaken."

"He's not the only one."

Marsh lifted the tea cup, gave the liquid a cursory blow, and sipped. He closed his eyes in appreciation. "He's worried that Takeshi and his boys will come back. I told him not to worry."

"Easy for you to say. We don't know what he'll do. Seemed like the boy was suffering from an inflated sense of self. I'm sure you popped his balloon a little, but I don't think he's going to appreciate you embarrassing him in front of his men. I think he'll be seeking revenge of some sort or other and likely to make another run at Dao."

"I don't doubt that."

I tried the tea. It was palatable, but barely. I prefer coffee.

"I've got someone watching the boat." Marsh gave me a look. "You're going to pay a visit to George Liu. We'll find out where Takeshi is most likely to be found alone. See what the old man thinks of his nephew and what he knows about all this juvenile delinquency. Then—"

A woman's head appeared around the open entrance to the

little room. "I'm leaving, Mr. Chapin. Do you need anything else? There are fortune cookies in the cabinets over there."

She was college aged and cute as a Japanese pixie.

"Thanks, Jen. We're fine. Smashing tea." He raised his cup to her.

She flashed a smile and waved goodbye.

While staring reflectively at the space she had vacated, Marsh said, "I've got a couple of people on Takeshi's trail. By tonight I should hear back if we have a firm fix on him so we can track his movements. I'll let you know where and when you can talk to Liu. Any questions?"

It looked like he had it handled as well as it could be. I was still nervous about my two old friends on the *Sweet and Sour*, that somehow Takeshi would circumvent Marsh's defenses, but I knew that whoever he'd assigned to protect Dao and Meiying was more than merely competent.

"Sounds like you've got it covered." I paused, frowned, my thoughts drifting back to the Wambaugh affairs. "Anything on Christopher yet?"

"As a matter-of-fact, yes. I just got a report late last night. The most interesting tidbit came from contacts at the Children's Network. My associate talked with several employees who frequent a bar nearby and was able to determine that young Christopher has been volunteering on and off for several years. He was working there when the abuse charges arose and was questioned on several occasions by the police. The charges were eventually dropped, but the rumor is that the center settled with some of the parties involved. Others say a troubled kid made up the charges to get back at a couple of the counselors for being strict with him. It's unclear what really went on. Just that Christopher was there at the time."

"Still, that doesn't really tell us much so—"

"And one young woman we spoke with, Mary Linn, said that

the woman you encountered at the Network the night of the shooting, Liz, I believe is her name, is particularly close with Christopher. Some of the other people there even thought they might be having an affair. But Mary Linn thinks she just felt sorry for him, a motherly concern. So, it's likely she was protecting him the night you showed up."

"Yeah. He probably escaped through the back door to an alley that leads to the wide world. There's nowhere he could have hidden inside. I had access to every room. How about Sarah? I understand she has volunteered there, too. Maybe Christopher got her involved."

"I was going to tell you. It appears, according to Mary Linn, that she was asked to leave by the executive director not too long ago. Mary Linn didn't know the whole story, but there was some tension between them. She said that Sarah had been volunteering for roughly the past year."

"Mmmm. That sounds like it needs a little follow up. Do you have any information about Scott, the executive director?"

"Working on it. We have the basic information, but now, after talking with Mary Linn, we're looking for more. Back to you soon. And, by the way, the associate I have following Christopher hasn't had much to report. In the past couple of days, he's only left the house twice. Once to go to Starbucks for a Frappuccino and the other time to buy a pair of jeans at Macy's at a nearby mall. Otherwise, he's stayed tight in the cradle of Mommy's bosom."

"Nicely put."

"You're still on for this weekend at the matriarchal abode?"

"Yup."

"Likely it'll turn into a total omnishambles."

"Omni-what?"

"Clusterfuck. Bo's a trooper for going along with it."

"I'll owe him big-time. Thanks, by the way, for covering the expenses."

"You owe me big time."

"I expected to forfeit a pound of flesh."

"Your flesh is not what I'm after."

"That's a relief," I said. But whatever favor Marsh ended up wanting was the least of my worries. I knew there was a better than average risk that by Sunday night I'd be locked behind bars, waiting impatiently for my friend's attorney to bail me out.

NINETEEN

I didn't gamble much, but when I did, Blackjack was my game, and I usually did okay.

Except when I didn't.

Sometimes, mostly, the dealer has the advantage and sitting down for more than a few minutes is a recipe for flushing hard-earned cash down the loo.

But I wasn't here to gamble.

It was the first time I'd been back to Poe's Pirate Cove Casino on Treasure Island in San Francisco Bay since the tawdry events that led to Frankie coming into my and Alexandra's life. It was the only good thing that had come out of that sordid case.

I imagined that Poe knew I was here. One of his eyes in the sky above me had probably spotted me the moment I entered and identified me as the thorn in the side I'd sometimes been to Poe.

Perhaps I had delusions of grandeur or and inflated sense of importance.

Or a paranoia justified by experience.

I turned to look at the reason I'd driven out here.

Speed Weed looked a bit like one of the dazed, aging hippies you see on College Avenue near the university in Berkeley. Lost in a haze of pot and memories of the halcyon days of flower power and righteous protest and unlimited guilt-free sex.

But while those trippy wanderers were now in their 60s and 70s, Speed was twenty years younger, but possessing that subtle not-quite-all-there affect that had you searching around him for where he'd mislaid his joint.

He was short and paunchy, with a little bouffant hairstyle—a blond, gray-tinged, pitched-forward semi-mohawk, which made an interesting contrast with the bald spot featured at the back of his head. Thick Elvis Costello style black-framed glasses sloped down his pug nose, accentuating pudgy cheeks.

He wore black loafers, slacks, and a white shirt with a purple vest festooned with exploding fireworks.

His eyes, a light green, had a surprised quality, as if he was having a hard time believing the reality of the world around him.

Q had told me where to find him and said his gambling problem was an open secret among local music professionals. He'd also mentioned that, according to his friends at bars and clubs throughout the city, Speed had been acting even more erratically than usual. There was talk of increased drug usage, probably cocaine, and gambling losses piling up with money he couldn't afford to lose.

I was biding my time, observing his actions, trying to figure out how deep in the dump he was.

His surprised eyes skipped around the table like a hummingbird looking for just the right dose of nectar. HIs fingers twitched constantly, as if he both couldn't wait to pick up his cards and, at the same time, was deathly fearful of finding out what fate had in store for him.

He was losing.

In the fifteen minutes that I'd sat beside him, playing two

hands with an average bet of fifty dollars per, he'd given Poe's house almost a thousand dollars.

In the same time, playing ten dollars a hand, I was down thirty bucks.

He wasn't a terrible player, but he had a tendency to push his luck when doubling down on soft hands when the dealer showed a seven or eight.

A sign of desperation. I didn't think it was a lack of experience or skill. There was a needy quality about the man, and that was never a good characteristic in a Blackjack player.

I felt for him. I've been around addicts of all sorts, some of them family and friends. Some hit bottom and get better, some don't. It's never pretty, for the addict or those close to him.

But I wasn't there to help Speed deal with his life problems, and I was afraid he wasn't going to run out of money as fast as I was going to run out of patience.

My chance came when the dealer, a grandmotherly black woman with sturdy features and a ready smile, pulled her third blackjack.

Speed muttered, "God damn," and his palm slapped the table.

"Would that he would," I said.

"Huh," his eyebrows raised, and his quicksilver eyes took a close look at me for the first time.

"God," I said.

He nose-lifted his Costello frames, his eyes narrowed. "God?" he repeated, as if he'd never heard the word before.

Oh ye of little faith.

"Damn it."

Speed was now profoundly puzzled. His whole body kind of swayed away from me, and he looked down at the two cards face down on the table in front of him, perhaps deciding whether glancing at the cards or me were the more dangerous option.

"I need a break. Can I buy you a drink?" I tried.

He looked up at me, still mystified. "I'm playing cards. My luck is about to change."

"I don't doubt it, Speed. But have a drink anyway. They'll still be waiting for you when you get back."

"How'd you know my name?"

"Come with me and I'll tell you."

I LED HIM TO THE PIRATE'S COVE TAVERNA, A BAR DIMLY LIT WITH fake candles and strings of Christmas tree lights centered on a bar in a lagoon fronted by a gangplank. We sat at a booth in a dark corner of the room with a large, half-melted candle in the shape of Captain Hook's hook in the center of a craggy walnut table scrawled with pirate words like Yarr!!, Arg!!, Dungpie, Hornswaggle, and of course, Savvy?

It was so realistic I felt like I was about to get seasick.

A waitress wearing a red bandana, billowy black pants, and a white peasant blouse, took our order. Speed had a Manhattan, and I ordered a coffee.

After our beverages were served and we were alone, Speed said, "You know me?"

"Of you. About you. But not the real you."

"What the hell are you—"

"Tell me about Sarah Swan."

"Who are you?" He sniffed, wiped his nose. Sniffed again.

"Max Plank. I'm looking into Sarah's shooting."

"You a cop?"

"Nope. Hired by somebody close to Sarah to investigate."

Speed twirled the cocktail glass around in his hand, took a sip, eyed me over the lip of the glass. "Don't have to talk with you."

"No, you don't. But I don't see why you wouldn't. I understand you had a relationship with Sarah. You were her manager and her boyfriend. Even if you broke up, I assume you don't harbor any ill will toward her." I picked up my coffee mug and took a sip of the black brew. It was strong, which I liked, but it had been sitting in the pot too long, leaving a bitter taste.

"She screwed me." He paused, chewed his lower lip with his teeth reflectively. Sniffed again. Wiped his nose with the back of his wrist. "Upset me. Sorry to see what happened to her. How's she doin'?"

"Improving. It'll take some time, but it looks like she's going to be okay."

"Good." He didn't sound overjoyed, but some people have a hard time expressing their emotions.

"When's the last time you saw her?"

He twisted his mouth to one side, his eyes glancing up toward the ceiling. His fingers drummed the table top. "Don't know. Maybe six months ago. The Black Canary. Checking out an act and she came in with her boyfriend. A young kid way out of her league."

"Red hair?"

"You got it. Anyway, we exchanged pleasantries for a few seconds. That was it."

"How about before then?"

"Hadn't seen her since the trouble we had. No reason to. Wasn't managing her career. She wasn't in my bed anymore." He closed his eyes and took a deep breath through his nose. "Hard on me for a while. Hurt being betrayed like that. On both fronts."

I couldn't really see what Sarah had seen in him. If Christopher was out of her league, Speed shouldn't have been in the same solar system.

"I understand that you sued her."

"Bullshit."

"But you threatened to."

"You know how it goes when you breakup. Everybody says

things. Never sued her, but maybe should have. She owed me. In more ways than one."

I tapped the table with my forefinger. "It sounds like you had plenty to be angry about. Are you sure that the last time you saw her was six months ago?"

"Fuck yes. Sure as shit." He sniffed. Sniffed again. Wiped his nose again. He drained his glass, grabbed hold of the table with both hands, and started to rise.

"I've got a few more questions—"

He reached his feet, stepped out from the booth, turned back to me. "Plum out of answers."

"Too bad. I was hoping to keep your name away from the police for a while longer."

He stopped mid-stride, did a quick one-eighty, and followed up with an unfriendly glare. "What are you saying?"

"Simple. You're right, you don't have to talk with me. I can't force you. But you will have to talk to the cops. At the moment, far as I can tell, you're not on their radar. Eventually, they'll get to you, unless they solve the case first. Maybe it's worth it to delay that moment of reckoning for a little while. That's up to you. All I can say is that I have Detective Marley on speed dial. Before you reach that Blackjack table, he'll hear the name Speed Weed for probably the first time in his life, not to discount the fact of your fame in certain circles."

"Got nuthin' to hide."

"Didn't say you did."

He sighed big time, making sure I realized what a total pain in the ass I was. "How many more questions?"

"A few."

He slumped back down into the booth and put his hands flat on the table. Immediately they started twitching. I stared into his eyes. His pupils looked dilated. He sniffed a couple more times. Rubbed the back of his hand across his nose vigorously.

Maybe he had a cold. Either that, or a deep affinity for sucking white powder up his nose.

"Hurry up," he mumbled.

"You're sure anxious to throw more of your money away."

"None of your business. Ask your questions."

"Where were you the night that Sarah was shot?"

His hands calmed. He glanced over my shoulder. Sniffed a half-dozen times, wiped his nose, squeezed his nostrils between his thumb and forefinger. "With a woman."

"All night?"

"Don't know. Don't know when she was shot or when she left the stage. Guess it was soon after she finished her show?"

I nodded.

"Doesn't matter. We had drinks. Dinner. Went back to her place. Didn't leave till morning."

"Who was she?"

He shook his head. Shrugged his shoulders. "Doesn't matter."

"Will she verify?"

"Sure."

"Can I talk to her?"

"Nuh-uh." He clenched his fingers into his palms. Relaxed them. Clenched again. "Save her for the cops if they come. Trust me. She will."

I had little doubt that if there wasn't a woman, there would probably be one when the time came.

"Okay, Speed. I've got one more question or, really, comment." I paused, trying to phrase it as delicately as I could. "I don't think you're telling me the truth. It's obvious that you were furious with Sarah for what you considered to be her double betrayal. You lost a stream of income and the possibility of much more if she makes it, which we both know, if there's any justice in the world, she will. And you lost her as your girlfriend. That's gotta hurt. So maybe this was eating away at you. The unfairness of it all. Sarah owed you. You weren't going to let her get away with it..."

I talked slowly, watching his reaction. He was staring at his hands, brooding. His fists stayed clenched tight.

"...and with all the coke you were doing, you weren't exactly thinking straight, you—"

His right fist shot out suddenly. I jumped back reflexively, his knuckles grazing my cheek. I grabbed his wrist with my left hand, steadied my grip with my right, twisted his arm upside down. He yelped, groaned, swore. I twisted a little further.

"Ouch, man! Hurts," he whined.

"You going to behave?" I held his upper arm in a vise.

He nodded vigorously, his eyes closed in pain. I let go of his arm, and it plopped hard against the table. He groaned and cradled it against his chest, rubbing the wrist with his other hand.

I let him have a few seconds to consider the state of the world. "You weren't thinking straight, and the anger kept building. Maybe you got high or had too much to drink and decided to confront her and, at the last second, not thinking, you took along a gun. You waited for her at the back of the club, and somehow, being there, hearing her great performance, her gorgeous voice, made you realize how much you'd lost and you wanted to make sure no one else, especially a young kid way out of her league, was going to benefit, so you burst in the room and shot her."

I waited, letting my words sink in. He was hunched into himself, gritting his teeth, in pain or anger or panic or some combination.

"That pretty much how it went? Tell me and you can take off. I won't even tell the cops. As I said, they'll find you sooner or later." I wasn't being honest with him but didn't feel any compunction to.

He dropped his hands to the upholstery, bolstering his body up and out of the booth. He turned away, stopped, turned back to me. "Making any calls?"

I let the question hang in the air between us for a while, suffering his angry eyes. "No. Are you going to answer me?"

"Don't like you. Everything you said is bullshit." And with that, he went off to make Poe an even richer man.

I sat there for a little while, sipping my coffee, and musing on if I really thought all the stuff I'd made up about Speed had any basis in reality.

TWENTY

The rain battered the already beat-up, peeling, grapevine-wrapped window frame. The glass itself was cracked, the panes foggy with failed insulation. The rain sounded like the flapping wings of angry birds.

Q was making coffee in the little galley kitchen next to the breakfast room where I sat with a plate of blueberry scones he'd whipped up that morning.

The cottage he rented was small but immensely charming in its late ramshackle life. It was decorated with old, not to say antique, furniture salvaged most probably from garage sales or local dumps. Still, everything was neat and clean and orderly, not like the typical bachelor pad, although you'd never refer to Q as a typical anything.

He was telling me about his name and his mother.

"My mother was white, Irish. She named me Quentin Quincy Quinn. My father, a black man I never met, had no say in the matter. Oona, my mother," he turned to me, waving the French press in his hand, "was a fan of alliteration, although she couldn't have defined or identified the word. She liked poetry, Doctor

Seuss especially, and e. e. cummings. She couldn't understand much of what old e. e. meant, but she loved the way the words and symbols were arranged, liked the way they bounced up against each other on the page."

He poured two Black Canary mugs full of the dark brew, put them on a tray along with matching red containers of sugar and milk and brought them over to the table. He put one mug in front of me, along with the sugar and milk. I nodded, added a small dollop of milk, and took my first sip. I smacked my lips and smiled at him.

He sat down across from me and continued, "You ever see *The Quiet Man?*"

"John Wayne."

"Maureen O'Hara," he said.

"Beautiful woman."

"Oona looked quite a bit like her. Her heart was almost as pure as Maureen's too."

"Sounds wonderful."

"She was. For a long time. I gathered she really loved my father and missed him terribly. They'd been together for about five years before I came along. I was an accident, she said. He'd always made it clear he didn't want to be nobody's father. That he wished he'd never had one himself. A week before I was born, Frederick, Oona told me he was named after Frederick Douglas, told her that he was going to do me a favor and disappear. Far as I know, she never saw him again."

The angry birds kept battering the window. Q held my eyes over the coffee cup. I didn't think there was much to say, so I didn't.

"He was her one and only. But she wouldn't even show me his picture. Because she respected his wishes. He didn't want me to know him. But course, being a stupid kid, I was desperate to find him. I needed to know what he looked like. When she left me alone, I searched every inch of her room, every damn inch of that little run-down house. Found nothing. She always kept her purse with her, though, and hid it so's I couldn't find it when I had the chance. Till one day when I was about thirteen and she was really sick with the flu, half out of her mind with a fever. I found her purse and found the photo in her wallet. He was wearing a Marine's uniform. He was black as coal, much darker than me. I studied his face. I didn't know what I was looking for. He looked fine. He had a sly smile, like he had a secret."

Q's eyes had a faraway quality, seeing that photo in his mind's eye.

"I memorized that picture. For a long time afterward, I'd search the faces of men on the street wherever I went, hoping to find him. But I never did. Whatever secret he had went to his grave with him."

"Is your mom still alive?"

"She been gone for a long time. Later on, when I was a little older and pretty much impossible to control, she got involved with a drinker. She started drinking herself, trying to be something she wasn't. It got pretty bad. Before she died, she went to AA and stopped. Went back to Jesus. She got a little crazy about that, too. But we were okay by the end."

He paused, smiled broadly, shook his head. "Good old Irish Oona. I was mostly lucky to have her be my mom."

We sat there in silent tribute to poor Oona, who'd had it hard but survived. Just like most of us. She'd had good times and bad and had a good man, a son, to show for her efforts. And maybe Frederick had been right to deprive Q of his father. I didn't think so, but he probably knew himself better than I did.

Q put down his coffee cup and said, "Mighty fine coffee if I don't say so myself. And wait till you get a mouthful of those scones." He picked one up, took a bite, murmured, "Hmmm mmm."

I raised my cup to him, took another sip.

"Tell me about what Speed had to say for hisself."

I did. He listened with his eyes flat and steady on me.

"Speed is weak. He's got no moral compass. And he's always desperate for money cuz of his gambling habit. And cuz of the Big C. Man like that, with those weaknesses, capable of anything."

"I agree with you, Q. Wondering if there's anything more you can find out about him through your contacts. Like where he was that night. If this woman he claims to have spent the night with really exists."

He got to his feet, moved back into the kitchen, opened a drawer, took out a pack of cigarettes that read English Ovals. A small matchbook appeared in his right hand, and he tore free a match, flicked it nonchalantly against the strike pad. It burst into a tiny flame, and he cupped his fingers, lit the cigarette, and dragged in a big mouthful of smoke. He sighed and released it through his nose contemplatively.

"Maggie Stevens or Jesse may know. Jessie used to be his girl-friend, and I think he confides in her. I'll check around some more."

"Good. Let me know." I took a bite out of one of the scones. "These are good."

He waved his chin up and down while taking another drag on his English Oval.

"Have you thought any more about the roses?" We'd discussed it as Phoebe had also told him about her concerns.

"No clue about that. I guess I knew about her not liking roses. But never really gave it a second thought. Someone sending her twenty roses has to mean something, but not to me. The note seems harmless, but strange. Wouldn't know who to ask about it other than Phoebe girl, and we already know everything she does. Was me, I'd talk to Rachel about it."

"Why?"

"A hunch. She don't like roses either."

I had the scone at my lips again, but stopped, as if somebody had just shouted that it was laced with arsenic.

"What?"

"Yeah. Kinda funny. Last time somebody sent Sarah a dozen roses. It happens every now and then. Anyway, somehow it came up in conversation while Rachel was waiting for Sarah to come out from backstage after a show. I mentioned about the roses, and Rachel told me that, just like Sarah, she didn't like them. Funny, uh? Both of 'em."

It was funny.

But not hah hah funny.

TWENTY-ONE

S cott Tripp agreed to meet with me at an espresso bar inside the Flora Gardens Nursery Center, a distinctly different place offering strange plants, unique decor, and funky pottery.

It was only a few blocks from the Children's Network offices and the Black Canary. I got there a little after eight a.m. and ordered an espresso, sitting at a wooden stool beside the lovely black-topped espresso bar and across from a beautiful big fica of some sort.

Outside I'd passed an ancient, decrepit black Pontiac that had been converted into a terrarium with wild plants and bushes filling the open trunk and hood and passenger compartment.

San Francisco never ceases to surprise with eye-popping discoveries. There's always something mind bogglingly new in Baghdad by the Bay.

Scott rolled in on his wheelchair as I was ordering my second espresso. He looked absolutely shocked to see me, and I had to ask him three times what he wanted to drink before he told me. I ordered him his double latte, heavy on the cream, and brought it to the small, round glass-topped iron table he'd parked his mode of transportation beside.

As soon as I sat down, he shook his head and said, "You lied to me."

I had fibbed. I told him I represented a wealthy investor who had decided it was time to give back and was interested in donating to the Children's Network. I was thinking of Marsh, and he certainly fit the bill of my description, other than the fact that he had no interest in giving anything back.

"I apologize. I thought you might not meet with me if you remembered me from the night I came to search your offices after Sarah Swan was shot."

"You'd have been right."

"Ergo…"

"I don't see why I should talk to you now."

"A free latte?"

He sighed.

"Interesting place." I lifted my espresso cup and waved it at the surroundings.

He didn't respond for a while, just sat there staring at me, trying to figure out where I was coming from. Finally, he took a sip of latte and murmured, "Mmmm. That hits the spot. I come here just about every morning. Starts the day out in a tranquil, meditative way that helps me face the rest of my day."

"I guess it can be pretty trying…troubling…working with the kids and what's been done to them."

He nodded, took another sip of latte. "Yes. Worthwhile. Rewarding, but tough at times."

"How long have you been there?"

"Since the beginning. I started it. It was my idea. Got a few grants and help from some generous patrons. That was almost fifteen years ago now." He shook his head again, like he couldn't believe how fast time flew by.

"Beside you and Liz, how many people work there?"

"Two others employed full time. Plus our bookkeeper. The rest are volunteers, more than twenty of them at any one time."

"How about management?"

"Just me, really. We have a board of directors, of course. I report to them." He paused, frowned. "I doubt you have this much fascination with our management structure. Why are you asking all this?"

"Of course I still love you," a woman at the table nearest us whispered. "It was nothing, really. Just a fling."

The emaciated, acne-scarred, woman sitting across from her wasn't buying it. She shook her head and looked away.

Despite the relationship drama, I refocused my attention. "Still trying to figure out what happened the night Sarah was shot."

"I don't see what that has to do with me or the Children's Network."

"That's what I'm here to ask you about. Sarah volunteered with you until recently for almost a year. I hear you had a falling out."

"How—" Tripp stopped, rubbed the back of his hand across his cheek. Took another sip of latte while deciding what to say next. "Doesn't matter," he muttered. "Yes, she worked with us. I am not at liberty to disclose why she no longer volunteers. It would be a breach of her privacy and ours."

"It just surprised me when I learned. Neither you nor Liz seemed at all concerned that someone you knew well had been shot. You didn't seem upset, surprised. Didn't mention to me that night that you knew her."

"You promised," acne-scarred face whispered, "that it wouldn't happen again."

I guessed they thought that their whispers prevented us from overhearing. Perhaps my hearing is acute. Either way, their secrets were now mine. But I intended to keep my lips zipped.

I allowed time for Tripp to think while I kept an ear tuned to the response due from the straying woman. Both took a long time, but cheater spoke first.

"The heart wants what the heart wants."

"You mean the pussy," acne-scarred spat out, a little louder than a whisper now.

"We don't disclose information about our employees or volunteers to the general public," Tripp said, staring at the woman who had just said pussy. I guessed it was the first word of their conversation that he understood. I had to admit, it was an attention-getter.

"Fine. I don't really get it. But you knew that Sarah had been shot. You knew her well. Yet there was no reaction at all to the news."

"I don't like your inference."

"I love you," the cheater whispered with strong emotion.

"I'm not inferring anything, just making an observation that struck me."

"I love you too, Squiggles," acne-scarred responded, her voice breaking with a similar intensity.

Squiggles?

Tripp glared at me. He didn't seem to find the word squiggles to be off-putting like I did. "We're getting nowhere. In the work we do, I've learned not to give too much weight to an individual's surface affect. An intensity of emotion may signal little while a blank stare and a rigid face may hide an ocean of feeling."

Wow. This guy was a font of psychological wisdom.

Squiggles and Acne clasped hands across the table and stared into each other's eyes.

"So that's what was happening with you that night. You were all upset inside about Sarah, but refused to betray the slightest hint of recognition or caring?"

"What's the point, Mr. Plank? Just come on out and say what you mean."

The problem was I sometimes don't mean what I say or say what I mean when I'm interviewing suspects. I can't say that I have a whole coherent theoretical framework, like Freud or Jung. It's more a seat-of-the-pants adaptable approach that depends on the suspect, my mood, my experiences, and pure gut instinct. In this case, my gut was saying that Scott Tripp was full of it.

"Liz told me that no one entered your offices that night after Sarah was shot. She said it was impossible. But I never asked you the question. Did you see anything unusual that night? Were any of the volunteers on duty that night? Did anyone show up unexpectedly?"

"It was just Liz and I that night. Not another person until the next morning as far as I know."

"As far as you know," I repeated, nodding my head up and down.

Notes from the William Tell Overture, the theme song for the TV show, *The Lone Ranger*, started playing, and Tripp fished his cell phone out of a holster strapped to the armrest of his wheelchair. He had a brief conversation curtly rendered with multiple yes's and no's and then returned the device to its holder.

"I have to go. Please don't bother me again. The police have questioned me fully about that night. I have nothing more to say."

I nodded.

He spun the wheelchair, and I muttered, "You're welcome."

He paused and gave me a quizzical look.

"For the latte. I know you meant to thank me, so I did it for you and responded in kind."

"Jeez," he said and rolled away.

Squiggles and Acne were still holding hands and smiling at each other, betrayal be damned.

TWENTY-TWO

I found Frankie in Alexandra's living room, curled up on the floor with a bag of Doritos trailing chips across the floor. She had tears running down her cheeks, hugging Red to her chest. The cat was meowing, none too happily.

The TV was on. Billy Crystal was rushing through the streets on New Year's Eve trying to reach Meg Ryan and tell her he'd finally realized what an idiot he'd been and how much he loved her. I immediately thought of the scene where Meg fakes an orgasm in a restaurant to prove to Billy that women are adept at propping up and fooling the male ego.

I was hoping that this wasn't what had made Frankie so sad. Maybe she was crying tears of joy for the fact that Billy had finally realized what was so clear to the viewer for the whole movie.

I knelt down next to her and said, "What's wrong?"

She kept Red in his uncomfortable noose at her chest but reached and arm up and wrapped it around my neck, smushing my face down into her shoulder. Don't let anyone tell you thirteen-year-old girls aren't strong.

My heart melted. Sorry, it just did.

No kid has ever made me feel the way this jackal has. It was unnerving. I can't say I liked it much.

I whispered again, "What's wrong, honey?"

"Jack," she mumbled, her lips against my neck. "Jack Rubio."

A new name. "What's wrong with Jack?"

"I hate him."

"Hmmm."

"He laughed at me." She pulled away, lifted the cat from her chest, and deposited him on the carpet nearby. Red scampered away, afraid she'd change her mind. She brought her feet into her thighs in a semi-lotus position and started playing with her toes, keeping her eyes down. "I was doing a skateboard trick for him, a nollie I've been working on. There was a rock on the ground, and it hit one of my rollers and I fell."

I reached under her chin and examined her face. There was a big purple bruise on her chin. I took her arms in my hands and examined the length of them. A few more bruises, a large Band-Aid on the back of her arm. "Mrs. Fenway, the school nurse, patched me up. She said to be careful, which she says every time. She should think of something else to say. There's another big cut on my leg, but it's okay. Only hurts a little bit anyway."

I thought it probably hurt more than a little, but she was a tough nut. She'd had to be, having had to endure what she had in her thirteen years. She was dynamite on that skateboard, but accidents were part of it, and I wasn't going to add to Mrs. Fenway's glib advice.

"So this Jack jerk laughed at you?"

"Jack isn't a jerk. I like him." She made a face like I'd just forced a spoonful of Brussel sprouts into her mouth. "I hate him."

I dug her. Wished I hadn't missed the more innocent days, her single digit years. But I knew that hers hadn't been as innocent as they should have been.

"Jack probably didn't mean to laugh. Boys, you know?" I said.

"Yeah. Max, I do. I really do," she said with a tone of voice belying her age.

We sat there for a moment while she examined her wiggling toes.

"He kissed Jessica Stern."

Ah, we'd arrive at the crux of the matter and the tears.

"Where?" I asked.

"Right on the mouth."

I'd put my foot in my mouth.

"No, where'd you see them?"

"On the bench at the park behind the school."

"I see," I said, nonsensically.

"I saw," she said. "But they didn't see me."

Before I got confused, I shifted. "So, you like Jack?"

"And hate him." Her eyes trembled. A single tear escaped her right eye and trailed slowly down her cheek.

I was way out of my element. What could I say that would make her feel better and not worse?

"Do you want to talk to Alexandra?"

Her eyes lit up, she wiped her cheeks, and nodded eagerly.

"Let's see if I can find her." I dearly hoped she was available.

I SAT AT THE KITCHEN TABLE, NURSING AN ALMOND MILK AND A vanilla biscotti, across from the living room where Frankie had been in an intense conversation with Alexandra for almost a half hour. There had been more tears but smiles and laughter too.

Alexandra told me that she was finally coming home next week. And not a moment too soon. I missed her, but, more importantly Frankie did. There's only so much a semi-surrogate father figure can do for a pubescent girl, after all.

I reviewed my conversations with Speed Weed, Scott Tripp, and Phoebe and Q, trying to cull out synchronicities and links, hoping for that ah hah moment that would solve the mystery and the complex motives behind it.

But nothing cohered, just a bunch of facts and opinions, incidentals that might eventually lead to something more important, more relevant to the case, but for now left me feeling exhausted, tired, and frustrated.

There was a knock on the front door. Alexandra's friend, Tabatha, had come to stay with Frankie while I attended the biggest party of the society season.

TWENTY-THREE

The heavy rain had started mid-afternoon and hardly let up a lick since. Looking out through the van window, the Wambaugh estate's sharp rectangular edges blurred, and I imagined it as some Manderley-like hothouse harboring awful secrets threatening all who entered.

I was cramped and hot, despite the cold and wind lashing the wavering trees outside, in the back of the catering van, stashed on a little bench seat between some Hors d'oeuvres, at least a dozen, including a salmon-ricotta concoction that Rope Rivers had recently invented, and desserts—a massive collection of sweets—from chocolate truffles to brandy bites.

I'd been sitting in the back of the truck for more than an hour while Rope and his gang unloaded food and supplies into the vast reaches of the Wambaugh kitchen and dining areas.

I'd discovered, through Rachel, that Mrs. Wambaugh was a huge fan of Rope Rivers. He was one of San Francisco's most prominent semi-celebrity chefs. I wouldn't be surprised if eventually they gave him his own TV show, as it seemed to be the natural course of things in celebrity-obsessed La La Land, which was now an apt description for folks not only residing in L.A. but applied just as well to binge-watchers in Lincoln, Nebraska or Garden City, Kansas.

It turns out that Mrs. Wambaugh's admiration for Rope bordered on idolatry, so I coaxed Bo into offering his services for a dinner party at the palatial estate of Rope's number one fan. Bo had called her out of the blue, feigning that he'd had a bright idea, that throwing a dinner at her house would be a great advertisement for the restaurant and for the blossoming fame of his chef. Bo promised to take care of all the details and to offer the affair free of charge, if Mrs. Wambaugh promised in return to invite all her rich, socialite friends and let her contacts in the society press cover the event.

She'd been flattered, overjoyed, and anxious to introduce all her friends to the fabulous young chef who she would now count as one of her intimates.

In truth, Bo didn't want nor need the attention for his restaurant. It was already one of the more popular places in town. I knew I owed him one and had promised to go and have a talk with my niece, his daughter, to see if she'd open up to me about any problems in her marriage. Not a chat I was looking forward to.

It was a little past six p.m. and dusk was in the air. I had to wait until it faded to black and the party was in full swing before I could escape my confines.

I'd expected that Marsh would be in on this little caper, but he'd left me a voice message saying he was going to be unavailable for an unspecified period of time. It was inconvenient, but not unusual. Every once in a while, Marsh disappeared for days, if not weeks. He always came back and refused to talk about where he'd been. I assumed that he did work for some deeply secret government or private club or other clandestine and borderline-nefarious organization, but when I tried to question him about it, the only response I got was an enigmatic smile.

I was as close to him as anyone on Earth, his best friend in fact, and since he had no long-term lover, although his young live-in Tom was still auditioning for the role, you'd think he would want to unburden himself.

But you'd be wrong. Marsh was Marsh. And you had to leave it at that if you wanted to be in his life. Some day he might open up, tell me all his deep, dark, soul-tormenting secrets, but I wasn't holding my breath.

I couldn't picture anything tormenting Marsh's soul. I couldn't picture him having a soul.

I opened up the latest James Lee Burke, Dave Robicheaux mystery and continued reading, engrossed in Burke's lyrical prose while I waited for night to fall fully. Or is it fully fall?

UPSTAIRS IN THE WAMBAUGH RESIDENCE, THE NUMBERLESS ROOMS and their adjoining hallways seemed endless and full of too much quiet.

I'd entered the house through the kitchen about an hour after the party started, after Bo signaled it was clear of any family members. There was a back stairway off the kitchen that led to the upper floor and all its bedrooms.

The lights were off, so the only illumination came from the starlight filtering through the occasional window in a cubby, or an open bedroom, or several small skylights punctuating the ceiling in an orderly geometry.

Dim and shadowy, but enough to navigate without bumping into the walls or tripping over any creatures lying in wait.

From below, the low thrum of a vast throng reverberated in my shoes. A loud shout, a raucous laugh, the rattling clink of ice in a cocktail glass occasionally reached my ears.

A faint smell of perfume—flowery, fruity, a little stale—along with a slightly sour ammonia smell drifted around me as I passed an open doorway disclosing another unused bedroom. I'd passed five of them so far with no signs of life. I was heading toward the northwestern corner of the house where Mrs. Wambaugh's master bedroom lair was located.

Marsh had gotten a copy of the house's architectural blueprints from twenty years ago. I hoped that she used the room on the plans that had the initials MB drawn in the center.

I passed another room, this one's portal shut tight. I pressed my ear against it for few seconds but could hear nothing.

I continued on, my heart gently bumping against my chest. I was used to this kind of thing by now. I didn't know if others of my relative ilk found it necessary to trespass on occasion, but it seemed to be one of the necessary hazards of the job, an imperative every now and again if you wanted to get insight into people's secret lives. The only way to get information required to solve a case, or save a life, perhaps your own.

Not a pretty thing to admit, but like many ugly truths, it was true nonetheless.

Or at least that's how I justified it to myself.

I was alert, but not overly fearful, cautious but not panicky.

Finally, I reached the end of the hallway and faced another closed door. I put my ear to this one and got the silence I expected. I knew Mrs. Wambaugh was down with her guests, reveling in bragging rights to Rope Rivers.

I hoped Rope kept himself in check. He had a low tolerance for bullshit and a high likelihood of saying whatever the hell he felt like saying. I'd asked him to please be nice to Mrs. Wambaugh, until at least after he was sure that I was gone.

"Nice," he said, as if it the word was a poorly prepared soufflé.

I knocked softly three times on the door, while glancing back over my shoulder to look down the empty hallway.

I opened the door and stepped inside, closing it behind me.

THE ROOM, OR RATHER, ROOMS, WERE BIG.

There was an anteroom with a glittering mirrored ceiling and a white marble floor leading into the main bedroom, the size of a standard professional basketball court.

The rooms were tastefully decorated with loads of inlaid Italian marble, expensive area rugs in muted patterns, and teak and mahogany accents.

Massive Tiffany lamps provided most of the illumination. Couches, loveseats, and chairs were all upholstered in beige leather with matching pillows. A baby grand Steinway piano took up one corner of the room and a giant golden harp another.

The bed was massive, round, and elevated on a high platform with modern sleek lines, plain and simple in its oversized luxury.

Next to the bed, light poured into the dim room from the skylight above a bathroom bigger than Q's house. You could have bathed one of Caligula's Roman legion in the jacuzzi tub.

On the opposite side of the bed was a gigantic closet stuffed with Mrs. Wambaugh's clothes and a separate room for a shoe collection worthy of a queen.

I found the computer in a little office beyond the main bedroom. It also had a marble floor and plain white walls, a teak and walnut loveseat, and a business-like desk with a comfy black vinyl chair on which a twenty-seven-inch iMac sat at rest.

I sat down, paused, listened intently for a few seconds. Nothing but the low hum of the party down below.

I woke the Mac up and started exploring files and folders.

It didn't take long as it appeared Mrs. Wambaugh didn't spend a lot of time online. Not too unusual for a woman of her generation. Especially one as rich as she was and who probably had a secretary and a bookkeeper and an accountant to take care of her mundane financial affairs.

There were photos of Christopher and Rachel, mostly taken in the past few years at various parties and charity events. None from their childhoods, but digital photos weren't taken as much around back then. I expected to come across folders full of kiddie shots when I searched the rest of the room.

I combed through her emails on AOL. There were a few message trails involving clubs and organizations she belonged to —Garden Club, the Republican Party, the Sharon Heights Gold and Country Club, the Menlo Circus Club (looked like they played Polo there). The only evidence of online shopping were occasional Amazon orders for books or office supplies or protein bars, a standing order.

I put the computer back to sleep and looked around. The desk had two side drawers, and I started with the top and smaller one. Pens, paper clips, blank notepads, envelopes, and some loose photos, grainy and faded shots of what looked like Hawaii. Most of the photos were of Mrs. Wambaugh twenty or thirty years younger. She wasn't attractive, even as a young woman. I didn't hold that against her. There were plenty of unattractive men and women who were admirable and wonderful human beings and who found love and sex and fulfillment.

In a couple of the pictures, she stood beside a handsome, large, muscular man probably five to ten years younger, with a full head of brown curly hair. He towered above her, his arm cradling her shoulder. He looked both surprised and sardonic, out of place but content to be there.

To put it bluntly, looks-wise, he was out of her league. Not all that extraordinary, but usually it goes the other way. Old, ugly men with power and money attracting younger, finer females.

I slipped one of the photos into my coat pocket.

The larger, lower drawer was full of hanging manila files.

They were all labeled: Home, Medical, Utilities, Phone, Projects, Contractors, and the like. I fumbled through each file, there were about twenty of them, finding nothing of other than passing interest, until, one folder from the last, I withdrew one labeled WF.

Inside I found what I'd been looking for. It wasn't a huge stash, just a few papers regarding interactions with the elusive William Fogerty, husband and father. And only one of them was important as it disclosed his address, a penthouse at the Palazzo Resort Hotel in Las Vegas, as of eight months ago when Mrs. Wambaugh had sent him a letter. Conveniently, a photocopy of the letter itself was clipped to the back of the folder.

I skimmed it, stopped, caught my breath. Went back to the beginning and read the whole thing. I took out my phone and snapped a photo of the letter and the address, making sure the print was large enough to be legible. I tidied up the file, put the folder back in its proper place, and closed the drawer.

I sat there for a moment thinking. The risk of coming here had paid off. These crazy law-breaking live wire acts often don't. I had what I needed, an important part of the missing puzzle. More importantly, I knew what my next step had to be. Soon as I wrapped up a couple of loose ends in here and found someone to watch over Frankie, a road trip to Sin City was in the offing.

My eyes fell upon a pile of receipts pierced savagely by a spike stick at the rear of the desk, almost hidden by the computer. I pulled them gingerly up and free of the spike, and as I quickly sifted through the papers, there was a slight shuffle of steps outside. I froze.

The muffled twang of the doorknob turning, the mild *thrwoosh* of the door opening. I leaned my head around the office doorjamb in time to see light from the hallway spill in a rectangle at the entrance to the bedroom.

I couldn't have picked a worse place to be interrupted. There was no place to hide. I could only hope she wasn't heading back here.

Should I stay, or should I go. The Clash's song lyrics played through my mind along with the layout of the bedrooms. Without thinking further, I danced around the office wall adjacent to the closet and disappeared inside.

Mrs. Wambaugh, marching toward her bathroom with single-minded purpose, didn't catch my fleeting shadow.

I hid in the furthest reaches of the closet, behind heavy winter coats unlikely to be of use to her that evening.

Still, I ran through logical explanations if I was discovered inflagrante delicto.

The list was short and pathetic, and I put it out of my mind while listening for approaching footsteps. I could hear her in the bathroom. She was humming. It was Sondheim's, *Children Will Listen.*

I reassessed my view of the woman. She had some taste after all. Sondheim and choosing me to help her solve this case were at least two gold stars on the right side of the merit ledger.

She left the bathroom. Her footsteps moved toward me. But she went right past the closet and into the office. I winced, feeling the big stack of receipts in my right hand. Maybe she wouldn't—

"What the—" she almost shouted, stopped. Silence momentarily.

"God damn it. Who's been in here?"

I thought about making an all-out run for it. I was pretty fast. She'd never catch me. If I put on one of her elaborate hats and a heavy winter coat, she'd never be able to identify me—

"Rachel!" she spat. "That girl better not..." Her voice trailed off. She rose, and I heard the chair bang against the desk. Mrs. Wambaugh stomped out of the room, moving quickly, a woman on a mission.

I stepped out of the closet. Looked at the wad of papers in my hand. Oh well, no use putting them back now. I shoved them inside my coat pocket and followed Mrs. Wambaugh's trail out.

But instead of stomping, I glided stealthily.

ONCE IN THE HALLWAY, I HAD ANOTHER DECISION TO MAKE. MY plan had been not only to invade Mrs. Wambaugh's privacy but Christopher's too. But I didn't know which room was his, and that might take a little time to determine.

I didn't know whether the old lady would confront Rachel now, in which case the two women would probably be back up here shortly.

But I decided that the confrontation would most likely wait until the party was over as she couldn't tolerate an embarrassing scene at this important event, especially with society reporters there and all the gossip that might hit the papers tomorrow.

I figured Christopher's room would be as far away from his mother's as he could manage. Nevertheless, I checked each doorway that I passed and found them all to be neat, clean, dust free, and empty of all but barely used furniture.

I found Christopher's room exactly where I expected. At the opposite end of the hallway from Mom. Once again, I paused for sounds of approaching steps before I took a deep breath and shut myself inside.

His room was as stark as hers was elaborately modern. A nice oak bed and desk set anchored the space. There were photos of Christopher playing baseball and tennis. Some trophies and ribbons, mainly for tennis. A few family photos, the three of them in Disneyland when they were much younger, or in front of a lakeside resort. I saw no photos of his father. There were lots of photos of Christopher and Rachel though the years. Playing together, sitting together on lawns, or at the beach, or at dinner tables of various sorts. In some, they were toddlers holding hands.

In a prominent place next to his computer, there was a striking photograph taken on the tennis court outside at dusk, a lovely orangish hue created by the setting sun.

Christopher smiled with his arm wrapped protectively around his sister's shoulder, an enigmatic look on her face.

I sat down at his desk and started searching his MacBook Air. I moved quickly. I found what I expected to, but not much more.

He had some folders full of correspondence and bills in a drawer on the right side of his desk, just like his mother. I read through them all, forming a more accurate picture of the young man.

After I finished, I sat there for a couple of minutes thinking about what I'd found.

Then I rose and listened at the door. Hearing nothing, I slipped back into the hallway, just as someone switched on the light above my head, and Christopher Wambaugh appeared at the top of the stairs.

TWENTY-FOUR

W e stood there for a moment, our eyes parrying. He was perhaps fifty feet away from me.

For a moment, he looked confused and glanced back down the stairway. I feared he was going to call down for whatever cavalry was close at hand, but instead, he turned back to me and gave me a searching glance, as if to make sure I was really there. Finally, he blinked, curled his hands into fists and shouted, "Hey, you, what are you doing here?"

There was no apt response, so I didn't bother. Instead, I tried to recall the details of the house blueprint that was tucked inside my coat. The stairway back down to the kitchen was half way down the hallway, past the spot where young Christopher stood shooting daggers.

Well, nothing to be done about that. I marched forward with conviction. I've found that acting confidently sometimes intimidates your antagonists.

Sometimes not.

But I wasn't too concerned about Christopher. The jig was up, my presence no longer a mystery. Nothing I could do about that now. I just needed to vanish before any of the local constabulary was called.

I was sure to be getting a visit from them soon, but preferred dealing with them on my home turf. I was a little worried since Marsh was incommunicado and he usually provided the legal help in these instances, but I'd deal with that when the need arose.

Christopher watched me approaching and stepped directly in my path. I stopped when I was arms' distance from his chest.

"What are you doing up here? What are you doing in our house? You weren't invited to the party."

Two questions and a statement of fact.

"Christopher, I'm trying to help. You and your mother haven't been honest with me. You left me no options. I'm trying to protect Sarah."

"You have no right—"

"No, I don't. But you had no right to shoot her, Christopher, did you?"

He looked blindsided, but desperate times call for desperate words.

The party had gotten a lot louder, alcohol lubricating and disinhibiting inhibitions. Shouts and cries and raucous laughter along with the thumping rhythm of the Rolling Stones made it unlikely that any noise from up here would reach the celebrants below.

"A counselor and two kids identified you as being at the Children's Network the night that Sarah was shot." I was ad-libbing, but, by the look on his face, hitting home.

"I chased your shadow into that building; I just didn't know it was you at the time. And I just found the receipt for the gun you bought last month. I'm sure the police have identified the bullet and gun it came from and—"

He lunged at me, caught me in a bear hug, and we tumbled to the ground and rolled around in a chaotic tangle for a few seconds. I grabbed his shoulder and forced him away from me, angling my right arm so I could punch him in the midsection, but suddenly, he started sobbing, letting me go, folding in on himself.

I crawled away from him, watched him break down, fall apart. He kept murmuring, "I didn't...I wouldn't...you don't understand." He sobbed, wrapped his arms around his shoulders, rocking back and forth. "You don't—"

"Christopher!" Mrs. Wambaugh shouted from below.

I jumped to my feet, touched his shaking shoulder with my fingers for a moment, trying haplessly to steady him, then hurried to the stairs leading back down to the kitchen and out the back door.

Bo had left the motorcycle at the edge of the Wambaugh property, about a hundred yards from the house, near a massive sprawling oak tree that must have covered a quarter acre of lawn.

I jumped on the pedal, and the engine roared like a panther, settling back into that pretty purr that pleases me from the tips of my toes to the top of my head. Glancing back from whence I came, I saw a woman on the porch that ran the length of the front of the house. Mrs. Wambaugh stood stock still, her hands limp at her sides, staring directly at me.

I broke the exchange first, closing my eyes, shaking my head. When I opened them, she'd disappeared. I twisted my hand back and forth on the clutch, revving the engine, and turned my back and bike on her and Manderley.

TWENTY-FIVE

When my cell phone woke me up, I came slowly out of a deep sleep to find Frankie snuggled on top of the sheets against my right side. I was confused for a moment, not sure where I was, suddenly conjuring my boat, missing it, my rocking, soothing abode. I hadn't slept there in more than a week as Frankie was closer to school and better off here.

The phone kept ringing, and I cursed myself for forgetting to put it on airplane mode. I reached over the still sound asleep Frankie and picked it up.

I whispered, "Yes."

"You killed him," the voice said.

I held the smooth plastic receiver against my ear. Repeating the words in my head, trying to make sense of them.

I realized suddenly that the voice who'd uttered the ridiculous accusation belonged to Mrs. Wambaugh.

"You're going to pay, Mr. Plank. You took his life; I'm going to take yours."

She hung up her phone, and I was left holding mine.

I was lost. It didn't make sense.

But I knew exactly what had happened.

TWENTY-SIX

I left Frankie still asleep on my, or rather, Alexandra's, bed and called Bo on the phone in the kitchen.

It was just after two a.m.

He filled me in on the details of what I already knew.

Christopher Wambaugh had shot himself in the head in his room at approximately eleven p.m., minutes after I left the house.

The police were there, and all the guests and Bo and Rope and the staff were stuck there until everyone had been interviewed. They'd already questioned Bo and were huddled with Rope and his sous chef at the moment.

He answered my question before I had the chance to. "I didn't tell them anything about you being here. They didn't ask, so I didn't offer. Did anybody see you, other than my people?"

"I don't think so." Christopher was dead. I had reason to believe, despite the fact that she'd threatened my life, that she might not finger me for a breaking and entering charge. "Have you seen Mrs. Wambaugh?"

"No. I guess she found her son. She's been holed up upstairs since." He paused, breathed through his nose. "Do you have anything you want to tell me, Max?"

"No."

"Okay, then."

"Sorry about this, Fiddle. Had no idea it would get so messed up."

"Shit happens," he muttered. Then added, "It just seems to happen so much more frequently when you're around."

"Thanks, buddy," I said.

"Anytime," he said and hung up.

TWENTY-SEVEN

A couple of days later, it was confirmed by Detective Marley that the gun Christopher used to kill himself, a Glock 27, a popular choice for novices, was the same one that had fired the bullet fished out of Sarah Swan's gut.

According to the police, that clinched things. MMO, the three cogs of the not- quite-round guilty wheel. There was Motive—Sarah breaking Christopher's heart, Means—the gun that Christopher purchased, and Opportunity—his presence nearby, at the Children's Network, the night of the crime.

Of course, the latter hadn't been proven.

But as far as Detective Marley was concerned, the case was solved.

Far as I was concerned, I felt guilty.

Knowing that my confrontation with him, my goads and threats, likely put him over the top. There was no way around the fact that, whether he shot Sarah or not, I'd pushed the kid too far.

I'd have to live with that unseemly fact long after this case was solved or forgotten. I pushed the accusatory thoughts away. There'd be plenty of time to drown in my guilt later.

I still had some doubts as to whether Christopher had attacked Sarah that night, although if he didn't, then my culpability would be even harder to deal with.

What I'd found in Mrs. Wambaugh's WF folder had raised questions that went beyond the simple tale now being told in the local paper about a distraught and depressed boy attacking his girlfriend after she broke up with him.

I'd been busy while the ballistics and forensics pros were doing their work.

But I had one piece of unrelated business to attend to before I followed up on what I learned at the big house in Atherton.

I'D GOTTEN A TEXT FROM MARSH THE PREVIOUS EVENING, FROM somewhere in the space-time continuum, telling me that I had an appointment with Liu at his home on Russian Hill.

I texted Marsh back for further clarification, but he'd disappeared back into some black hole.

I had no idea what Liu knew about the meeting or the situation with his nephew or who I was or why I was there. But he'd obviously agreed to meet me, so I was hoping that Marsh hadn't strayed too far from the truth to get me access. From our sources, Liu hadn't made his money by nefarious means and wasn't actively involved with criminal elements. Nevertheless, I always kept in mind Balzac's dictum: *Behind every great fortune lies a crime.*

There was such a cynical realism behind that quote. It was perhaps not one hundred percent true, but close enough for this world.

I got to The Summit on Green Street, the name of Liu's thirty-two-story high rise, in time for the doorman to check my bonafides and direct me up to the twenty-second floor. I knocked on Liu's front door at exactly 9:02 a.m.

According to Google, he lived in one of San Francisco's most exclusive neighborhoods on one of the original seven hills, and in one of its most iconic buildings, designed by Joseph Eichler, the most influential architect in the Bay Area in the mid-fifties. Joe wanted to bring style and class, in the mode of Frank Lloyd Wright, to tract housing. Whether you like them or not, his designs are instantly recognizable with their post and beam construction, floor-to-ceiling windows, exposed ceiling beams, and funky atriums.

After knocking, I waited, stepping back from the door so I could be examined in the peephole. When I judged that relatively enough time had passed, I raised my fist again, but lowered my hand at the sound of something being dragged across the floor inside.

The doorknob rattled for a few seconds before a firm grip was established and the door swung open.

George Liu stood trembling, both hands gripping his walker. He was a short wisp of a man. A brown beret clung perilously to one side of his bald head. His desert sand-colored skin was pock-marked with age spots. His brown eyes were partially shielded beneath lightly tinted oyster-shell glasses. He was a seasoned member of the octogenarian club.

I smiled at him, introduced myself. He pursed his lips and nodded. He made an effort to lean back with the walker, but it didn't move even a centimeter. I stepped in and around, offering a shoulder to lean on. He mumbled something I couldn't under-stand, took my arm, and we inched slowly into the living room.

It was spectacular. Twelve-foot, floor-to-ceiling windows on all sides with views of downtown San Francisco and the fog-shrouded bay in the distance.

After what seemed like an hour but probably may have been closer to five minutes, we arrived at a round table with five chairs set squarely between the views of the TransAmerica Pyramid and the Bank of America building. One of the adjustable vinyl-covered chairs was set higher than the rest, and Liu indicated that he wanted to sit there. I guided him down into it and took the seat beside him.

He sighed as he settled in, coughed, and cleared his throat.

As if on cue, a stout middle-aged black woman wearing a kind of black Nehru-style jacket appeared with a tray carrying both tea and coffee, two bowls of steamed buns, and one of white rice.

As she put the platters in the center of the table, carefully placing an empty plate and cups in front of each of us, her eyes took my measure discreetly. I gave her a smile.

She shook her head almost imperceptibly from side to side, bowed, and left.

Perhaps she didn't like my smile, despite the sincerity behind it.

Liu cleared his throat again, pointed at each of the bowls in turn and said softly, "Pork, vegetable, soybean." Using chopsticks, he picked up one each of the buns and then, slowly, nudged some of the rice onto his plate.

I mimicked his actions, picked up the tea pot and, after getting his assent, poured him a cup. I poured myself a coffee.

He took a sip, then silently started working away at his breakfast. I took a bite of the vegetarian bun. It was delicious, as was the coffee.

I gathered the old guy wasn't interested in talking before eating so I occupied myself enjoying the breathtaking views of the most beautiful city in the country while downing four buns and a little rice.

As I finished the last of my coffee, Liu cleared his throat again, and said, "My nephew. Tell me."

I put my cup down. The jangle it made was jarring—I hadn't noticed how quiet the condo was.

"Thank you for the breakfast, Mr. Liu. What did my associate tell you?"

He dabbed at the corners of this mouth with a napkin, smacking his lips, making little bird-like gasping sounds. "He asked me if my nephew's actions regarding my investment with Mr. Dao had been authorized by me." He cleared his throat, smacked his lips again, mumbled, "Must tell Felice to steam buns longer still."

I waited a few seconds while he stared at his plate, considering whether to finish a half-eaten pork bun. "And did you?"

He raised his eyes to mine, blinking repeatedly. "I do not know what my nephew did. Mr. Marsh did not tell me. He sent you here. Tell me."

"Do your nephew and his family live here with you?" The place was huge, the room we occupied, encompassing the living and dining rooms and ultra-modern kitchen, had to be at least three thousand square feet. Long hallways branched off from the center north and south of us to what I assumed were lots of bedrooms and baths.

"No longer. Felice and I. Just the two of us."

The old man suddenly seemed sad, a pained expression settling on his face. Or maybe it was just the way the he looked after breakfast. I wanted to ask about when his extended family moved out, but it didn't seem relevant in the moment and was none of my business anyway.

"Please, Mr. Max, tell me about my nephew."

I felt restless. I stood, walked over to the glass wall, watched the fog drifting through the Bay Bridge spires and cables, a ghostly misty merging.

Einstein's theorem popped into my head: $E=mc^2$.

Energy is equal to mass times the square of the speed of light. Somehow the ethereal fog blending with the hard, manmade mass of the bridge seemed to embody the famous scientist's profoundly difficult equation. It made little sense, but neither did the theory.

Deep thoughts, my friends. Max Plank is known to have them, sometimes at the most inappropriate moments.

I took a deep breath and began to summarize the actions taken by Takeshi against Dao along with our countermeasures. I summarized as best as possible but spoke for several long minutes. Liu sat silently, listening I hoped.

When I thought I pretty much had covered all relevancies, I took one last long look at the fog and the bridge and rethought my linking of those juxtapositions to the most famous theory in the history of science. I could see no sense in my link.

I sat back down next to Liu and waited for his response.

He'd finished the rest of his steamed bun. He took a sip of tea, frowned, and said, "I was afraid. I should never have let them leave."

"Where are they living now?"

"Here. On the third floor."

"That's so close—"

"No. It is as far as China. I never leave this house. They do not visit. My brother, ever since he stopped working and his Jinjing, she dies, he is depressed. I send Felice down, and they tell her they will come. But they do not."

He closed his eyes, shook his head, smacked his lips, struggling to swallow.

He was old and weak physically, but I wasn't detecting any signs of the dementia or mental deterioration that his nephew had emphasized.

"So you haven't seen Takeshi in…?"

"Two months, more."

"And he wasn't acting on your behalf?"

"No!" Liu's voice sounded like broken glass.

"But you had to discuss your losses, your involvement with Dao, with your nephew."

"No," he said, his eyes meeting mine. "I told my brother. I was unhappy, but I did not blame Dao." He flashed a half-smile. "Maybe a little."

"You told your brother you were unhappy or mad at Dao?"

"Maybe," he said. "But Dao warned me. I decided that with his record, what I knew, that he could be trusted. I invested a little too much." He cleared his throat. "It was crazy."

"You lost a lot of money?"

"Oh, yes." He paused and flashed a mischievous smile. "But I have a lot of money still. I pay for this home and for my brother's home below, too. I will not run out of money before I run out of breath."

"So you weren't mad enough to try and retaliate to Dao in any way?"

"No. No. He did not cheat me. It was my fault. I was upset with him, but with myself too."

"Tell me about your nephew."

"I will not say he is a good boy. He has good qualities." He sighed heavily. "I should have sent him back to China, to Chengdu, where my family is. Perhaps…no…I am old. I do not understand. I want to blame America for Takeshi, for corrupting him. I want to blame my brother. He is a quiet man, much like men of his generation, Asian men with their sons." He touched the right side of his face with a trembling finger, frowned. "He tried his best with Takeshi, but he did not understand what needed to be done. And now he's given up. Some men are born with *E gui* —hungry ghosts inside, that they cannot control. That is Takeshi. He is fascinated by the Yakuza. He is a foolish and mean young man. I have talked with him, and he seems to listen. But I doubted. And now, with what you tell me, I can see that my words had no effect."

"I'm afraid that he will try again. I worry for my friend Dao and his wife. They live in fear now. And I fear for your nephew. My friend, Mr. Marsh, is a very dangerous man. Dao is his good friend. He will deal with Takeshi harshly if he threatens Dao again."

A long silence followed. Liu stared unseeing out the picture windows. I kept on trying to re-link that tenuous connection between Einstein and the fog and bridge to no avail.

Finally, Liu said, "Takeshi will not bother Dao again. I will meet with him today, even if I have to leave this house. I, too, know very dangerous men in this city. Someone in my business, the sale of and management of large properties, is involved with all kinds of men, men who one would rather not meet, but must. I have enriched a few of them, without wanting to. They will respond to my request for a favor." He closed his eyes again, and they filled with tears. He reached up with quivering fingers and wiped them away.

"Can you bring my walking machine before you leave?"

I propped it beside him, thanked him for breakfast and for his help. He fixed me with a steady gaze and said, "Takeshi will not bother you again."

I nodded and left him there, hoping that Felice, that sturdy, much younger woman, wasn't just his caretaker, but his friend. Like so many lonely old people in the big city, he needed one.

TWENTY-EIGHT

That evening, while I was preparing Frankie my famous cheesy cheese mac 'n cheese, I got a call that eventually led to a whole new understanding of the case and the crimes, and the secrets and lies running just beneath the calm surface of things.

At first glance, it didn't seem to be anything but another senseless death.

"How are you, Q?"

"Been better. Been a whole lot worse. Doing a lot better than our friend, Speed."

Then he told me about the poor bastard, and I began to think that there was truly something murderous about my approach to people in this case.

"When did it happen?"

"Last night, I guess. Woman, I know the girl, named Felicia, pretty black girl but a coke head. Don't know if she was dating him or supplying him. Anyway, she came to his apartment and found him dead on the living room couch. He was sitting there with his eyes open, staring at nothing. TV was set to *Jeopardy*. She called me before she called the police. I'd just called to ask her a week ago about Speed, after you asked me to check him out. I told her to call 911. She didn't want to. Told her they'd find out she was there anyway, and she'd be in real trouble, she tried to pretend she was never there."

"So you don't know if he tried to kill himself or it was just an accidental overdose?"

"Overdose. Heart attack. Killed hisself. All the same thing in Speed's case. He was on a spiral. Couldn't control anything in his life, including the gambling."

I remembered him sitting across from me at Pirate's Cove. The desperation in his eyes, the bitterness, the constant sniffing and nose rubbing. I knew whatever happened wasn't my fault. But my toughness with him surely hadn't helped. Thinking about Christopher and Speed, had I known more about their fragility, would I have handled them differently?

If I thought either one of them was on the verge of suicide, certainly I would have. But, lacking clairvoyance, I was never going to be able to predict who of my many suspects might be vulnerable.

Still, I couldn't help feeling like an asshole.

"The cops are probably going to want to talk to you if they find out Felicia called you first or if she mentions you contacted her about Speed."

"Yeah. Figured that."

"Let me know if they give you a hard time."

"Oh, they gonna give me a hard time. But it don't bother me no more. I expect it, dealt with it before. You don't get to be a black man my age and not figure out how to deal with the blue men."

"Tell them I was the one that got you involved. Let 'em hassle me."

"Maybe they're not gonna hassle nobody. Likely a simple overdose. Nothing that gonna cause 'em any trouble so they won't come botherin' nobody."

When I hung up, I noticed the mac 'n cheese was smoldering, starting to blacken in the cast iron pan, the secret of my recipe, along with olive oil and cracked black pepper. I grabbed the pan and got it off the burner and spooned the gooey stuff onto plates for Frankie and me and cut some French bread to go with it along with a salad with strawberry dressing.

We ate while Frankie took turns petting Red on her lap and stuffing forkfuls of mac 'n cheese into her mouth, talking about her day and the fact that she didn't really hate Jack so much anymore, that he could be nice sometimes, and that he'd told her she was the best skateboarding girl he knew, and she told him she was the best skateboarder, period. She talked excitedly about coming to the airport with me to pick up Alexandra this coming weekend. Red kept on snaking his face beneath her elbow, his tongue lapping the lip of her plate.

I listened, but my mind was reeling, considering the likelihood of both Christopher and Speed's demise being mere unrelated coincidences, remembering what I'd found in Mrs. Wambaugh's desk, and deciding I needed to ratchet up my game significantly to get to the bottom of things before anybody else died.

My thoughts were interrupted by Frankie's decidedly diplomatic comment, "I like your cheesy cheese mac 'n cheese, Max. I do. But next time, it'd be easier to just make it out of the Kraft box, right? A lot easier and…it's kinda hard to beat if you know what I mean?"

I did.

TWENTY-NINE

Rachel Wambaugh no longer looked like the same woman I'd met at the tea garden just over a week ago. Her hair was different, pulled back in a tight bun that accentuated her high cheekbones. Dark shadows, little nightmares, plagued her eyes. Her face, despite some additional makeup to cover it up, was drawn and pale.

She'd moved back into her mother's home, at least temporarily. I knew it wasn't safe for me to get anywhere near that house, so I arranged to meet her at Mr. Mayhew's Coffee & Croissant Shop on the main drag in Burlingame, the Eucalyptus tree capital of the world.

I'd been there once before, and it was a large, disheveled place with booths in nooks and crannies of the idiosyncratic layout that allowed for lots of privacy. Mr. Mayhew himself, who I'd met on my previous venture, was a smiling young Brit, who unashamedly favored 1970s era dress like bell bottom pants, brightly colored baggy shirts, and platform shoes. The shop itself was full to brimming with that era's hippie bric-a-brac. Posters of 70s icons—

Lauren Hutton, Margaux Hemgways, Woody Allen, Robert DeNiro, Jack Nicholson, and Gene Hackman—covered the walls.

We sat in the most isolated corner booth tucked behind a large rubber cactus and a life-size cardboard cutout of the monster from *Alien*.

A coed dressed in a tie-dyed t-shirt and bright red hot pants brought us full coffee mugs, along with the almond croissants we'd ordered.

I don't remember croissants being in favor in the 70s, but these were the best I've ever had, so I guess it didn't matter.

I looked across the table at Rachel. She was staring down at her plate, her fingers playing with the edges of it, turning the saucer ever so slowly.

"I'm so sorry about Christopher," I said, which I'd already told her on the phone. She hadn't responded then and didn't now. We sat in silence for a while longer.

Finally, she tapped her spoon against her cup, as if calling a meeting to order and said, "My mom blames you. She says you broke into our house. You talked to him. You harassed him." Her voice was flat, monotone. Her sentences weren't quite questions, nor statements-of-fact, but something in between.

"Your mother has cause to be upset. I did sneak into the house. I did try to get Christopher to tell me the truth." I felt guilty as hell, but lurched forward, ready to take my medicine. "I was tough on him. I had no idea…but that's no excuse. I thought he may have been Sarah's shooter. That's what I was focused on. It's what I do. Sometimes I get…" My voice trailed off.

"You shouldn't have broken into—"

"I didn't break, I snuck."

She glared at me. "You shouldn't have 'snuck' into my mother's house." She paused for a long moment, gathered herself. "But, Mr. Plank, you didn't kill Christopher. Maybe you pushed him too hard at the wrong moment. But you're not responsible for what he did. I'm guiltier than anyone. I should have seen the signs. I'd distanced myself from him, particularly since I got involved with Sarah. I knew how much that hurt him. But I didn't care."

She closed her eyes, her face a mask of anguish. "I was tired. Of him. Of my mother. Of being a Wambaugh. I needed to get away from it all. Sarah offered something different. A chance to start fresh. I'd spent years taking care of Christopher, I—"

She stopped, her cheeks reddening. "Shoot," she said. "Listen to me. I don't know what I'm saying. I..." She grabbed the fingers of her left hand with her right, twisting them into a knot, wringing them as if they were dirty, trying to get rid of a stain. Her face cratered, tears streamed down her cheeks, her body shook.

I watched helplessly. Reached my fingers toward her, stopped.

Our waitress appeared from behind the cactus plant, took one look at us, and veered away.

Rachel sobbed once, clenched her teeth. Cursed. "Damn him," she muttered.

Shaking, she dug into her purse sitting on the booth beside her. She found a wad of Kleenex and dabbed at her eyes and face. She blew her nose. Gathered herself.

"I'm sorry."

"Nothing to be sorry about," I mumbled.

I waited a little while longer before daring the questions I'd come there to ask.

"Why do you think he did it? What was going on in his life? The police have pretty much concluded that he shot Sarah and the evidence confirms..."

She sniffed, cleared her throat, and said with some authority, "He didn't. He couldn't have."

"He's your brother, so I understand. It's hard to think of him as doing something like that. But he had cause. He was in love with Sarah, and she dumped him. And then the two of you got together. Some men just can't handle that kind of loss and—"

"It wasn't like that..." She shook her head, started playing with her plate again. "He never had a real relationship with Sarah. It was totally one-sided. A friendship, not a love affair."

"Unrequited or not, it can have the same impact on the one who loves."

"No. I don't think so. Not this time. Not Christopher. He didn't love her. He tried to, but it was an act."

"I don't understand."

"I can't explain. Trust me. He was my brother." Her eyes bore into mine with such naked intensity that I wanted to look away. "I knew him," she said, her voice breaking into a fervent whisper.

"So, because you don't believe he really loved her, there wouldn't have been the passion necessary to try to murder her?"

"Yes. But also, he wasn't a murderer. He was a vulnerable, wounded, lost young man."

I'd seen that, felt it. That hadn't stopped me from going after him.

"Who wounded him?"

"My father. And me."

Ay, there's the rub. Back to the patriarch. I'd assumed most of this family's struggles arose from Mom, but maybe not.

I waited for her to tell me more.

"Dad was brutal. He could be charming. The world, society, found him charming. But he was a weak, pathetic man. To us, his family, he was..." Her voice trailed off, tears reappeared in her eyes. She hunched down, the muscles in her neck tightening as she tried to get a grip on herself.

"...he abused Christopher. He was always putting him down, making him feel less than. Dad lived off Mom, off the family business. He hadn't accomplished anything real in his life. It's hard to say about your father, but he was more or less a gigolo. I don't know if he loved Mother at all. But she loved him. She loved him too much. Anyway, I don't know why he seemed to despise

Christopher. But the verbal assault was constant. And he beat him, too. On a regular basis. By the time Christopher was a teenager, he was hollowed out, a shell of a boy, stuttering, withdrawn, afraid."

"He didn't seem that way when I met him."

"He got some counseling. I tried to help him all I could. He learned how to put a face on for the world. How to hide the hurt and pain. But inside, I don't think he ever came close to healing. A monster. That's the word. My father was, is, a weak monster."

Music had been playing at a low level, unrecognizable psychedelia, but now the volume rose and that avatar of all things flower power, Donovan, was singing that everyone was calling him Mellow Yellow, quite rightly.

"You haven't seen or spoken with him for years?"

She nodded.

"How did he treat you and your mother?"

"No better. He didn't hit my mother, but she knew not to cross him. She knew what would happen if she tried to intercede on his behalf. He never hit me," she said, and looked away.

"Do you know what it was like cowering in my room, hiding under my sheets, while my father went after my brother? I've... never been able to get the sounds, the cries, out of my head. When I can't sleep at night, I hear them all over again."

She stared into a corner of the room, remembering the everyday horrors of her childhood home. "I'm sorry. I shouldn't. I can't..."

"Why didn't—" I stopped, tried to put a plug in it.

"Why didn't we do anything? Why? Seven and nine-year-old kids? And he's big. Scary big. Knows how to use violence. He preys on weakness."

"What about your mother?"

She shook her head. "Like I said, she loved him. She needed him. She had all the financial control, but it didn't seem to make any difference. She pretended like nothing was happening. We never talked about it. She wouldn't listen if we tried."

"I'm sorry," I said and felt pathetic saying it.

Her features softened. "No one can understand really. No one who wasn't in that house. And there's only three of us left now. The last couple of days I've been thinking about going to see him. Finding him. Confronting him. Telling him that he murdered Christopher."

"Maybe you should."

"I'm afraid. He still scares me."

"What about your mother? Couldn't she help? She knows where he is. She could—"

"Mother is a lost cause. She made her decisions about her life a long time ago."

More Donovan floating in the air, singing about the impossibility of catching the wind and his lover's love again.

I didn't say anything for a while and neither did she.

We finished our coffee and croissants in silence, and I shifted uncomfortably in my seat. I told her that I was going out of town for a couple of days but asked if there was anything I could do for her.

"No. I promised Mom I'd go with her to make more arrangements for Christopher's services. It's going to be pretty private, but still there are things to do."

"Of course." I paused, thinking, remembering what I'd come here to ask her. "Rachel, I understand, like Sarah, that you don't like roses. It seems odd, and I was wondering if you could tell me why—"

"Oh, Max," she said, the muscles in her face twitched, trembled. She started sobbing, tried to regain control, but it was no good. She fell apart right there in front of me, and it took a long time before she was able to put the pieces back together again.

Once she did manage to get a hold of herself, she stood up, said, "Bye, Max," and hurried out of the coffee shop.

Later that day, she called me back and answered my question about the roses. Her voice was faint, and she sounded like a lost little girl as she told me the terrible truths she'd been desperately hiding.

THIRTY

It was a ten-hour drive from Alexandra's house to The Palazzo resort hotel in Las Vegas.

I left at ten p.m. after tucking Frankie into bed. Meiying, once again, had come to the rescue. Frankie treated her like the grandmother she'd never known, and Meiying, in response, like the daughter her and Dao had never been able to have.

I told them both I'd be back in a day and a half, at most.

I'd contacted Marsh through our "red phone," as we jokingly referred to it. It was actually a regular old iPhone that he'd given me. I'd been instructed not to use it unless it was the most urgent of emergencies. He'd promised that, in most cases, if I left a message on voicemail using that phone, he would return the call no matter how deep undercover he was.

I'd only used it once before in the four years I'd had it. That time, he didn't think the emergency was dire enough, just like this time.

Nevertheless, within three hours, I had the information I needed to go push forward with my hastily constructed plan.

Without bothering to check, I'd stopped at the garage Marsh

maintained on Van Ness Avenue beneath a dry cleaner he owned. I knew everybody there, so I had no problem securing the keys for my ride, a mint-condition navy blue '72 Ford Mustang. I'm not much of a car person, but Marsh raved about the ride. The garage held about twenty vehicles, from Aston Martins to Jaguars to BMWs along with vintage cars like the Mustang. He employed a part-time mechanic to keep them purring.

After checking traffic on my phone, I took the Bay Bridge to Oakland and then Highway 80 up past Richmond and Berkeley and onto Sacramento and into the Sierra Nevadas. Passing through Reno, I discovered, as expected, that the town fathers still considered it to be the Biggest Little City in the World.

From there, I picked up Highway 95 and rode that lonely desert road all the way into Sin City.

The desert had its own kind of stark beauty, but I had little appreciation for it that night. My thoughts kept on returning to my conversations with Rachel and Christopher and Speed and Mrs. Wambaugh and Scott Tripp and Q. Had both Christopher and Speed killed themselves? Were there deaths directly related to Sarah and the shooting, or might they have died of wounds delivered long ago?

I was still trying to make sense of how the mystery of the roses impacted current events. If the gift of flowers the day of Sarah's shooting was mere coincidence, or the key to solving the case.

Experience told me it was more likely the latter.

I only stopped once on the way, to get coffee and a protein bar at a truck stop just outside Hawthorne, Nevada. Although it was tempting, I passed on waiting for the town museum to open later in the day. It boasted the largest collection of inert ordnance— missiles, bombs, rockets, and, nuclear weapons—in the whole US of A.

I made a note tell Marsh about it. He'd probably want to make a special trip and take photos for his Christmas card.

I arrived at the Palazzo, smack dab in the thumping heart of Vegas, a few minutes after eight a.m. The resort was surrounded by the famous Strip's behemoths—The Mirage, The Wynn, Treasure Island, and I discovered, connected to The Venetian via the Grand Canal shopping complex, replete with gondolas.

The property was massive, labyrinthine, confusing. So, I pulled into the impressive Porte Cochere and handed my keys to the valet. An expensive way to go, but my time was short and my wallet full for the moment.

The kid who drove off with the Mustang, after expressing his delight at getting the chance to get behind the wheel of such a rare "beauty," gave me a slip with the number seven printed on it.

Maybe it was my lucky day.

I'd soon find out.

To face down a true monster, one might well need a little help from Lady Luck.

I ASKED THE FRONT DESK WHERE I COULD GET BREAKFAST, AND THEY directed me to the fourth floor and the Canyon Ranch Café, which promised to detox me with organic non-GMO ingredients. I felt a little offended that the reception area staff thought I was toxic.

I ordered steel-cut oatmeal, sweet potato toast, a bowl of blueberries, and a pot of coffee and kissed thirty bucks goodbye.

I ate slowly, savoring my food and the decent coffee, reading a Dean Wesley Smith novel on my phone.

At nine a.m., I took the elevator back down to the casino and sat down at a Blackjack table.

The crowd was relatively sparse at that time of day, but there were still a surprising number of people playing one-armed bandits and video slots.

Roulette and poker tables were less populated, with only a few sleepy-eyed diehards plugging away.

I had the table to myself and had fun, ending up winning enough to pay for breakfast after an hour of parrying back and forth with a smile-ready dealer. I left him a ten-dollar tip, and he wished me continued good luck.

It was 10:15, and I headed upstairs to the Canyon Ranch Spa. It was a state of the art facility and then some, including a full gym, a myriad of daily classes from yoga to Gyrontonic Expansion, a multi-sensory Aquvana water experience, plus massage, reflexology, acupuncture, shiatsu, ritual bathing and much, much more.

One-hundred-thirty-four-thousand square feet of more.

I'd read the brochure when I purchased my day pass for fifty bucks.

I flashed the pass at one of the white-frocked attendants and headed straight for the rock climbing wall.

WILLIAM FOGERTY SCRAMBLED UP AND DOWN THE SHORT WALL LIKE he was a lizard born to it.

He was naked from the waist up, wearing a pair of tight-fitting purple stretch pants. He climbed barefoot and without a harness. He must have gotten a pardon from the club because they normally required special shoes and double bind ins for would-be climbers.

But this was no mere mortal and, besides, Marsh estimated that Fogerty, or rather, the Wambaugh Companies, paid the resort over one-hundred-thousand dollars a month to live in the Chairman's suite, his home for the past two years. A bargain, I'm sure, for lodging that offered twenty-seven televisions, its own spa and gym, and a karaoke room. Somehow I couldn't picture Fogerty holding a little microphone and belting out the love theme from *Titanic*.

He was in his fifties, a time when normal men did not strip to the waist on a rock wall. But his body looked twenty years younger, long, lean like Marsh, but with more muscle. It took a lot to preserve a body like that at his age, along with a strong assist from nature.

I watched him scamper up and down the wall for twenty minutes. The only other person around was a young, very fit, very attractive young woman who sat with a fixed gaze, holding a couple of white towels in her lap.

When he finished, he jumped down to the floor from halfway up the wall, landing like a graceful ski jumper, and trotted over to the woman, who provided an admiring smile along with the towel. As he wiped the sweat from his face and chest, he surveyed his surroundings, and his eyes soon fell on me.

I was standing twenty feet from him, with my arms folded across my chest, making no effort to conceal my interest. I dipped my chin and said, "Pretty impressive, Fogerty."

He narrowed his eyes, examining me. His study took a few seconds, before he determined that he didn't have a clue who I was. He dropped the towel onto the young woman's lap and came over to investigate further.

"You know me?"

Up close, he looked closer to his age. His skin was tanned, rested. I'm sure he got his fair share of massages and treatments, but the wear and tear, and wrinkles under his eyes and at the corners of his mouth could not be completely erased, even with Botox.

"Yes and no."

His eyes probed mine, and we had a moment together. I didn't like it. Maybe it was Rachel's story infecting my view of his character, but I didn't think so.

This was a bad hombre.

Judging from the expression on his face, I didn't seem to be his type either.

He glanced away, looked over his shoulder, nodded.

A moment later, a pair of hands clutched my shoulders smartly. I started to turn my head, but the grip tightened to the point of pain. I let it be.

"What's your name?" Fogerty asked.

"Plank. Max."

"Do you know me, Mr. Plank?"

"Like I said, yes and no."

The hands dug into my clavicle, and I winced. I moved my right foot farther right and my left foot back a step while the pain spiked. Handsy responded by moving a foot between my legs. I slammed the heel of my right foot down hard on his toes. His grip released right before he cried out. I danced away, my eyes on Fogerty.

Who smiled at me.

"I see," he said.

Handsy squatted low over his shoe, rubbing it and cursing. Muttering about how I should just wait. Hold on just one minute, God damn it.

After a few more humiliating moments, he stood, rolled his shoulders back twice, settled into a semi-Neanderthal stance, and took a step toward me.

"Enough, Waldo," Fogerty said. "Go."

Waldo, who was a big slab of meat in his thirties, gave me a dirty look, but backed up, spun, and disappeared.

"What do you want?" Fogerty said.

I explained myself, shading the truth.

He invited me up to the Chairman's suite.

THIRTY-ONE

N o use describing the suite in boring detail.
 Like I said, twenty-seven televisions, gym, spa, karaoke room. Gold, silver, stainless steel, wall to wall glass, stunning views.

Big wow.

Really.

What money can buy.

Fogerty made me a cappuccino from a fancy machine and poured himself a glass of white wine that probably cost more than my boat.

He told me to take a seat. I had a choice of a dozen in the living room overlooking the sprawling majesty and tawdriness of Las Vegas, from its glittering candy-colored heart, pumping relentlessly, its artery-clogged streets spilling into palatial estates, mundane suburbs, and shabby, desperate corners.

I took a seat at the large, fully-stocked bar.

There didn't seem to be anyone else in the suite, although my information said it had up to seven bedrooms and more than eight thousand square feet. No telling who might be hiding out in its far-flung reaches. Waldo had disappeared, but I assumed he was within barking distance.

"My wife sent you here?" he said, then took a sip of the wine, his tongue laving his lower lip.

"Indirectly," I responded, biding my time, but feeling a nasty itch inside me that I was dying to scratch.

"You have a problem answering direct questions, Mr. Plank?"

"Nice place you have here. Homey, in its own way. Donald Trump might find it lacking, but—"

"I'm losing my patience."

"Well, William, I guess, exiled to this far flung," I looked around, opened my arms out, "Xanadu, I'd think you would have cultivated patience. As nice as it is here, you're kind of on the periphery of things. You can't go near your family, or your wife's business. It must sting, just a little bit. I've been wondering what you do with your time…" I picked up my cappuccino, took a leisurely sip, and continued, "I would think patience, and boredom, would be your good buddies by now. I mean that rock wall is pretty pathetic as a pastime for a man of your age, despite your undeniable flair for scaling it."

Fogerty placed his wineglass down on the top of the bar, turned it once, positioning it exactly to his liking. He put his hands down flat on the gleaming hardwood surface, looked down at his feet in contemplation, and said, "I'm just going to say this once. I don't know who you are or what you want. I'll give your one more chance to tell me why you are here."

He was irritated, but still in control. His voice carried a hint of the beast, but he was still a polite, card-carrying member of civil society.

I thought about what I wanted. The call of the wild or just some answers to my questions? Was there any chance that this man would tell me what I wanted to know? Would he unburden himself of his guilt, his role, his actions, in the whole terrible mess that he'd made of his own family?

I reminded myself that I was in the lion's den, the devil's lair, and that I had no weapons with me, save for my wits and my hands, for which I often tended to have too high a regard.

No telling what my opponent held at the ready here in his not-so-humble abode.

I considered all this as the timer ran down—I could almost feel Fogerty's coiled spring tension threatening, just a bar skip away.

I bit my tongue, prepared myself for what might come out of my mouth.

"As I said, I was hired by your wife," I said, and as I did, I decided to tell him the truth, mostly, from the point three weeks ago when the Mrs. stepped onto my boat until yesterday, when Rachel told me the secret at the heart of her family's hidden life. Once I reached that point, depending on how he responded to the rest, I'd decide how to proceed.

I realized that I didn't even know if the man was aware of Christopher's suicide, although I guessed someone must have contacted him by now.

I told the story, summarizing, omitting some details, but leaving nothing of importance out.

When I got to Christopher, he didn't respond in any appreciable way, so I assumed he already knew or didn't care enough to have an emotional response.

While I spoke, he'd wandered out from behind the bar and settled into a high-backed chair in the center of the room that was angled toward the windows. He sipped his wine, glancing out reflectively on greater Las Vegas from time to time.

"Is that it?" he said, when I finished.

"Pretty much."

He stood, the empty glass of wine clutched in his right hand,

and walked until his nose almost touched the massive floor-to-ceiling wall of glass. He kept his back to me.

"Isn't this something?" he said.

"That it is."

"Do you know what it took for me to get here?" He turned to face me, waved his hand in an arc, encompassing the room, all the lush accoutrements that wealth brought. "To get all of this?"

"Magic, right?"

He looked perplexed.

"You married into it. Your wife's great-great granddaddy made his fortune off Wizard Oil. He was a carnival barker without peer, giving the poor and suffering all the hope they could stand. Maybe you're a little similar to him. Something of a con man. You saw an opportunity to get rich quick without effort. Seizing on the neediness of a lonely, rich woman. You married her for her money. Doesn't seem like hard work to me."

The truth will set you free is my motto.

I felt the glass more than saw it whizzing by my ear before shattering against the back wall of the bar.

All the tiny hairs on my body started tingling.

The beast had emerged without warning. I wondered if when he attacked Christopher, it happened the same way, like a flipped switch, one minute light and bright, the next total darkness. With Rachel, it had to be different. His actions there were pure premeditated evil.

My time here, I could tell, was short.

I can take a hint, perhaps not as well as the next guy, but still.

He acted like nothing had happened. He moved back to the bar, poured himself another glass of wine, and downed in a single gulp. He poured himself another and gave me a tight-lipped smile. "Her father paid me to take her out." He smiled, remembering back. "Said that his daughter was lonely and hadn't had a date in years. Said she was a good girl, but too focused on the business."

"How'd you meet him?"

"At a big society event. I was working with a service that provided dates to mature women of means. We shared a drink, and he offered me the job."

"The job?"

"That's what it was. Strictly confidential between him and me. She was always trying to please the old man, get some of his love and attention. She adored him but didn't understand him and so she feels unloved to this day. I understood him. He did care for her, but she never knew." He paused, glanced back out to the blaring light of the midday sky, took another sip of wine, and smacked his lips. "I kept it a secret until long after we were married and the old man was dead. She didn't believe me at first. I tried to convince her that it showed his concern for her. How he was trying to make her happy, in his own way. When I saw how devastated she was, I doubled down. Told her that it had been a setup, sure, but I'd fallen in love with her. I could see that she was starved for it. Seeing what the old man had done to her. It gave me my opportunity…"

His eyes were far away, back in time, the wheels of his mind churning, remembering, congratulating himself on taking advantage of his big break. He may have never told this story before and had been dying to let someone else know what a brilliant strategist, a smooth operator he was. Pulling a fast one, the big score, over on the wealthy magnate and his poor, ugly duckling daughter.

"He never expected me to marry her, but by then, I'd even fooled him. I saw my chance. She loved me, needed me. It worked out all around."

"Still doesn't seem like hard work."

"Shit," he said, turning, moving back into the center of the room where he faced me. "I wasn't attracted to her. You've seen her, haven't you? She looks like that actress in the *Wizard of Oz*, the Wicked Witch of the West. I've been to bed with some homely women, but those were one- or two-time deals. She was crazy about me and wanted me to feel it, show it. For months, I had to act like I wanted her. I deserved an Academy Award. It was acting for real."

My skin was crawling. I didn't want to listen, but I needed him to keep talking.

"I had to convince her and her father that I'd really fallen for her and wasn't just after the money. He still made me sign a prenup, but I figured I could work with that. As soon as he kicked the bucket, I got her to tear it up." He laughed. "That bitch will do anything for me."

I couldn't believe he was telling me all this so brazenly. I'd been right speculating how much this luxurious exile had affected him. The pent-up resentment and anger for the compromises he'd had to make for mere money. Lots and lots of mere money.

"What about your children?"

"What about them? I never wanted them. She begged me, but I refused. She lied to me. Said she was taking the pill. So, Rachel came along. I was furious, but nothing I could do about it. Rachel wasn't half bad. A beautiful girl. Not like her mother at all. Takes after me."

"Christopher?" I said.

"Didn't like him. He was a selfish little brat. A momma's boy. And his mother lied to me again. Told me she was on birth control. I was furious that time. I actually went out and got a vasectomy after that. I wouldn't trust the bitch anymore."

Jesus. I've listened to a lot of miserable, SOBs, but William Fogerty made me want to puke my expensive breakfast up all over his fancy carpet.

"Isn't she still paying for all this?" I waved my hand in a circle.

"Sure. She's still crazy about me. She comes and sees me at least once a month. I don't sleep with her anymore, but I let her hang around. She's like a moon-sick puppy. Believe me, Plank, it gets old. Don't tell me I haven't earned all this." He paused, shook his head, moved to the bar, and poured himself another glass of wine. He downed it in a single gulp and poured another. "Only thing she loves as much as me is dear dead Daddy's company. She'd do anything to make sure nothing hurts Wambaugh. It's double insurance for me. If she ever decides she doesn't love me, I've still got her and Christopher over a barrel. I've earned what I have here and I'm not giving it up."

"What do you mean?"

He fixed me with a steady gaze. "I've said enough. The rest is none of your business. In fact, why am I even talking to you?"

"You're not the first who's ever asked that question."

I sized him up, thought about what to say next, decided to go for broke. "Did you hire someone to take a shot at Sarah Swan?"

Surprisingly, he didn't throw another glass at me. Not even his shoe, which I was half-expecting. My question seemed to calm him.

He waited a beat before responding. "Who is Sarah Swan?"

He was good. Or clueless.

"You've never heard of her?"

He shook his head.

So, I told him about Sarah. Her involvement with Christopher and Rachel and his wife's obsession, along with the attempted murder.

"I don't keep track of my children's love lives. I don't know why Marjorie hired you to investigate this singer. To be honest, I no longer have any contact with my children. As to the shooting, this is the first I've heard of it and hopefully the last."

I stifled a remark that might have led to deadly projectiles aimed for my head.

"We're finished," he said, walking to the bar and placing his glass down sharply.

He acted as if nothing of consequence had happened between us. That the despicable behavior he'd revealed toward his wife and family was no big deal. That throwing a glass at someone's head out of the blue was not worthy of an apology or an explanation or even a brief mention.

"I have a couple more questions."

He rolled his eyes. "I'll give you two more minutes as long as you don't act like a jackass."

He was asking a lot of me. I was pretty sure I was going to disappoint him. I took a long breath through my nose to calm my own inner animal and work up the gumption to say what needed to be said. I felt like I owed it to Rachel, and to Christopher, to at least attempt to make this man acknowledge what he'd done.

And, despite his claim of complete ignorance around his children's lives, I still couldn't shake the feeling, the suspicion, that he knew much more than he was saying. He wasn't going to answer my questions directly, so I had to rattle his cage, so to speak.

"Did you know about Christopher's suicide?"

"I was contacted, yes."

"Your wife. The police?"

"Who cares?"

"I wonder if the police might have any interest in the kind of father you were to Christopher."

The quiet in the room seemed to suddenly deepen, the stillness sharpen. A long moment passed.

"What are you talking about?"

"I understand you were pretty tough on the boy."

"This is none of your—"

"In fact, you beat him viciously, repeatedly. You didn't father him; you tortured him."

He loomed large in the center of the room. He had all the trappings of wealth and power but had done nothing but deceive and manipulate to get them. He was a pathetic monster, a gross perversion of a human being.

"You belong in jail, William. Not here. This is not your due."

He closed his eyes and smiled. "I'd advise you to leave right now, Mr. Plank."

"Unfortunately, Christopher never had the wherewithal to confront you. You'd beaten it out of him. And now he's dead. You're safe, the statute of limitations protects you."

"Waldo," he barked. "Terrence."

Heavy footsteps in a hallway nearby.

"But not with what you did to Rachel. She can still bring charges against you. Your daughter, who you sexually abused all those years ago. I think she's ready, William. Maybe you're going to end up in that jail you belong in after all."

My friend handsy Waldo, crew cut, left tackle for the Vegas Also-Rans, and Terrence, a cougar-slick slice of svelte devil-may-care, both carried what appeared to be .38 specials with silencers attached.

Fogerty nodded to them and then to me, and the two men moved in on me. I turned to face them, crouched in a fighter's stance.

"Stop," Fogerty called out to his men. They froze in place ten feet from me. "Lay down on the floor, flat on your stomach, and put your hands behind your back."

"Unlikely," I said, opening and closing my fists, readying for a little of the old *ultra-violence*, as Alex in *A Clockwork Orange* terms it.

"Waldo, shoot him in the knee cap."

I dropped to the floor, put my hands behind my back, cursing under my breath, wondering where-oh-where in the world Marsh was.

Terrence bound my wrists with a nylon zip-tie. They dragged

me to my feet and took a firm grip of each of my shoulders respectively, but not respectfully.

I still had my legs and feet free, but I didn't like my odds if I tried something fantastical.

Fogerty moved in on me. His face full of malice, his eyes as dead as any stone-cold killer.

When I get really scared or nervous, I tend to talk a lot, so I started in.

"All those roses you gave Rachel after you violated her. What the hell was that about?"

He was up close and personal now. His face had a nasty scowl on it, beads of sweat poured from beneath his hairline. The first shot was a right uppercut that slashed deep into my solar plexus, followed by a crossing left to my ribs.

I cried out, keeled over. Gasped for breath. Waldo and Terrence kept a grip on my shoulders and pulled me back up straight.

Fogerty knew what he was doing. He probably had his own boxing coach.

He gripped my chin in his hands and forced me to look directly into his eyes.

"Have you been talking to Speed?" he hissed. "You're as stupid as that drugged-out loser. Do you want money, too?"

The mention of Speed rocked me as much as his fists had. I tried to wrap my mind around the fact that he knew Sarah's agent and had been involved with him. That money was involved. But Fogerty kept talking and throwing me off balance.

"You have a young lady in your life now. And a woman friend. More than a friend. I believe she is in Vietnam at the moment, on assignment. You miss her. Taking care of the little girl is hard in your line of work. But you don't mind. You've come to care for her."

Staring at me, he delivered another rocking punch to my

midsection. I heard an odd screeching sound, followed by a guttural grunt as the boys held me stiff and steady.

"Your family, such as it is. You can't be too careful. Life is treacherous. One wrong move and those closest to you might disappear. Frankie, that's her name, right? And Alexandra. Such a pretty name. Such a pretty woman. It would be terrible to have that face harmed. Ruined."

Another shot from his left hand, this one just beneath my ribcage, the fist searching for my kidney. I grunted, then felt sick, about to vomit.

Fogerty stepped away and waited.

It might have been a minute, perhaps longer, before I felt like I might not lose my insides. Fogerty moved closer again.

I closed my eyes and mumbled. "I still don't get the roses. Why did you send them to Sarah the day she was shot? I can't...figure it out and..."

Another shot to my stomach silenced me, followed by two more. From what I can remember, he just kept punching. In the back of my mind, I wondered, or felt some relief that he wasn't going after my face.

If I survived, I'd still be pretty.

Soon though, I felt like nothing more than a worn-out punching bag, and sometime after that, I was no longer aware of anything at all.

THIRTY-TWO

I don't know how they got me out of the Palazzo undetected, but when I woke, I was sitting, or rather, leaning, behind the wheel of Marsh's Ford Mustang in the middle of nowhere.

It took me a while to figure out who I was, let alone where. My vision blurred, my brain foggy, my tongue parched and foul with stink.

The passenger seat had dried vomit all over it.

There was a note taped to the steering wheel.

According to the old analog car clock, it was just after nine p.m.

The center of my body felt like it housed a demon witch's black cauldron of boiling sulfurous oils.

My ribs ached, vortices of fiery pain.

My head throbbed like the inside of Max Weinberg's drum kit.

Other than that, I felt pretty good.

I sat there breathing in and out. Taking an inventory of my whole body. There didn't seem to be any blood, at least externally. It was possible that I was leaking inside, and that it would kill me sooner or later.

The attack had been brutally focused to exact the most pain without a trace of evidence that it had ever happened.

When I felt I could stomach it, I tore the note from the steering wheel and brought it up close to my eyes. It was typed in large print on plain white paper.

REMEMBER. YOUR LOVED ONES.
Stay out of Vegas for a while.
Out of the Palazzo forever.

I OPENED THE CAR DOOR, ANGLED MY BODY CAREFULLY UNTIL I WAS able to place a foot on the unmaintained dirt road on which the car was parked.

I hunched over, felt like I was going to throw up again, dry heaved a couple of times before the gag reflex quieted.

I closed my eyes and steadied myself.

I reached up and grabbed the top of the door, hauling myself up onto my feet. My knees wavered, threatening to collapse. I steadied myself against the car until my head stopped swimming.

I looked around.

In the distance, beneath a couple of hazy street lights, I glimpsed the highway.

Around me, the shadows of mesquite bushes and cactus and dead Joshua trees as far as the eye could see.

I turned three-hundred-sixty degrees and spotted the towering spires of Las Vegas hotels perhaps ten miles away.

I stumbled around to the trunk and found a couple of rags. I opened the passenger side door and cleaned up the vomit as best I could, stifling the urge, the gag reflex, to add to the mess. Marsh would not be a happy man. I'd blame it on Fogerty and let nature take its course.

I tossed the rags over my shoulder and got back in the car. It still stunk but so did I.

The bumpy unpaved road did a number on my roiling stomach. When I hit 95, I turned south back toward Vegas. I didn't intend to violate Fogerty's restrictions quite so soon, but I needed a drink of water and knew it would be closer in this direction than back north and home.

When I had sated my thirst, I'd head back to San Francisco. I had a lot to think about and ten lonely dark hours to do it in.

THIRTY-THREE

I got back to Alexandra's place a couple of hours after Frankie caught the school bus. I called Meiying and verified that nothing but the normal had occurred while I was gone.

Dao took the phone. "Max, have you heard anymore from Takeshi? Marsh said not to worry, but he is gone."

I recounted my meeting with George Liu and his promise to take care of his nephew.

When I finished, Dao didn't respond, and I listened to him breathing quietly for a while. "I understand you're still worried. I don't blame you. I'm going to follow up with Liu today and make sure Takeshi isn't a threat. Marsh has posted men to watch over you."

Still silence.

"If it makes you feel better, why don't you set sail? Waters are calm. Take the boat out to the Farallones and anchor offshore. Takeshi won't be able to find you there. Call me in the morning. I'll let you know what Liu says."

"Okay, Max. Maybe so."

The House Speed Weed rented off Taraval in the Sunset District was attached on both sides, a typical row house, an amalgam of Spanish Colonial and Craftsmen style, blending the worst elements of each. It was in a state of disrepair and badly needed a paint job.

I hoped Speed had gotten a break on rent. Only in California could a simple, relatively small house in a nondescript neighborhood be worth more than a million dollars.

Late morning, there was no one around. The front door was tucked in an alcove surrounded by worn brick. Stone planters with stale, dry dirt and no plants filled the small space.

I removed the lock pick set I'd retrieved from my boat and used it to open the pin and tumbler lock with the greatest of ease.

Inside it was cold, dusty, and unkempt. Like most bachelors, Speed wasn't a neatnik.

It was a small house, two bedrooms and a single bath. The furnishings were sparse. A couch and chair in the living room fronting a glass topped table with magazines, mostly music-related, and newspapers strewn across its surface. A newish flat screen TV.

The walls were naked, save for a large unframed painting of Duke Ellington and his big band wailing away that hung in the center of the living room wall.

The air in the house was stale, sweetly-sour, and slightly antiseptic smelling. Perhaps the remains of the medical examiner's visit to Speed's dead body.

The kitchen was a tiny room with all the necessities and a small breakfast counter. The countertops were Formica, in a pattern popular in the 1960s.

Dishes were piled in the sink, the stains of unfinished meals still stuck to their surfaces. The refrigerator held three beers, a hunk of cheese, and a carton of stale milk. It smelled of rotting bananas from the three blackened specimens I found in the produce compartment.

The bedroom contained an unmade queen-sized bed, a large bureau, a bedside table with a reading lamp, a copy of *Atlas Shrugged*, and a hairbrush. A Fender Stratocaster stood propped in a corner of the room next to a small amp. A Gibson acoustic guitar leaned against the end of the bureau.

Not a surprise that an agent, a talent manager, would be a musician. Oftentimes, it's a way to keep yourself in the game that you love so much.

I remembered my meeting with Speed at the casino, the shell of the man I found there. I tried to think of him in younger days when he might have loved music and played in a series of unsuccessful rock 'n roll bands.

Bo and I had been there, done that. I felt little nostalgia for it.

My mind wandered back to my mission. The bedroom was the place to start my search, so that's what I did.

I WAS STILL FEELING PRETTY TERRIBLE, LIKE I'D BEEN HITCHED TO A wild horse and dragged for long dusty miles on a gravel road. I felt like I was lumbering rather than walking. It took me almost an hour, with breaks to sit down and catch my breath, to do a thorough exploration of every nook and cranny of the bedroom and its small closet.

But I didn't find what I was looking for until I went to the kitchen for a glass of water. As I was sipping and looking around, I decided to explore right where I was.

I opened all the cabinets and searched the pantry. I opened the drawers beneath the counters and found nothing but what you'd expect to find: silverware, pots and pans, towels, plastic plates.

I stood up, felt a sharp pain in my side, grimaced, gripped my arms around my waist. I breathed in and sighed and dreamed of my eventual return to Las Vegas and my next meeting with William Fogerty.

I noticed the small cabinet above the refrigerator and reached up high. Feeling the pull on my sore ribs, wincing, I grasped the handle and drew the door open. At first it looked empty save for a dusty black exhaust pipe running near the top.

I was about to close 'er up when I noticed the edge of a manila folder laying on the bottom of the cabinet. I touched it with the tips of my fingers, drawing them toward me, and inched the folder out. I snatched it and sat down on the stool at the counter.

I took another sip of water and opened the folder.

What was in that folder didn't answer all the remaining questions I had.

But it surely satisfied most of them.

THIRTY-FOUR

As I was driving back to Alexandra's house, Phoebe called to tell me that Sarah was out of her coma. She told me that Rachel had slept overnight at the hospital and was with her still.

I banked the bike to the curb for a few moments to think about my approach to the two women. I'd planned on confronting Rachel alone later that day, but questioning the two of them together, although uncomfortable, was even better.

I did a one eighty on my bike and headed back toward Highway 101 and San Francisco General Hospital.

ONCE AGAIN, I FOUND MYSELF SITTING AT THE FOOT OF SARAH'S BED.

But this time, it was different as the patient was awake and alert. Rachel sat next to her on the mattress, holding her hand.

I'd learned that the doctors had started weaning her off the drugs inducing the coma a couple of days ago, and she'd come out of it the previous afternoon.

She looked a bit spacey and spoke slowly, pronouncing each syllable distinctly, as if she were practicing a new language. Still, she seemed coherent, bright, and happy to be back in this world.

I remembered the night I first saw her, the stunning singer lighting up a room full of adoring fans. I'd become one of them by the end of the first song.

I couldn't wait to hear her sing again.

"Sorry for showing up unannounced, but as soon as Phoebe told me you were awake, I knew I had to come and see the both of you. It's very important that we talk now."

Rachel nodded, her gaze unfocused. Sarah smiled weakly and said, "It's okay, Mr. Plank. Rachel told me how you reacted that night, how you tried to help. And how you've been working on solving the mystery ever since."

"It's been a big day. You need to rest," Rachel insisted. She turned to me and said, "What's so important? Have you found out who did this to Sarah?"

I ignored the slight edge of irritation in her voice, attributed it to her wanting Sarah to herself, finally after all this time.

"I went to see your father."

Her shock registered with a sharp intake of breath.

"God…what…why…you never said…"

"After what you told me, I didn't want to upset you further. I didn't know if I'd actually get to see him. Or if he'd even talk to me."

Sarah patted Rachel's thigh, tightening the grip on her fingers. "It's okay, Rach. He has no power over you anymore. Let's hear what Mr. Plank has to say."

Rachel stared at their conjoined hands. Sarah lifted her chin, looked gently into her eyes. "It's going to be okay."

Rachel nodded. Sarah looked up at me. "Go ahead."

Rachel kept her eyes everywhere but on me. I couldn't blame

her. It must have felt like the monster that had ruined her child-hood was back in the same room with her.

I summarized my time in the Chairman's suite. I didn't dwell on my being used as a punching bag. I didn't go into great detail about his callous attitude toward Mrs. Wambaugh and Rachel or his indifference to Christopher's suicide.

I did emphasize the fact that, despite his initial denials, he knew a lot about what had gone on here in San Francisco in the past couple of weeks. That it seemed a fair guess that he was involved in Sarah's shooting and perhaps even in Speed Weed's overdose. When she heard that, Rachel groaned and buried her face in Sarah's shoulder.

It was torture for Rachel to listen. By the time I finished, she seemed more like a recovering victim than Sarah did. She kept her face hidden in the crook of her friend's shoulder.

"I'm sorry," I said.

She didn't acknowledge my words, just stayed nestled in the comfort of Sarah's arms. Silent tears streamed down her cheeks.

I paused, watching the two of them, feeling like something was being withheld. Something left unsaid.

"I wanted to ask you both, again, about the roses. I talked to your father about them but got nowhere. I accused him of sending them to Sarah."

I had come to believe that the roses might be the key to solving the whole affair, like the sled in *Citizen Kane*. The ultimate mystery, the unknowable source, the unsolvable riddle.

The roses were the reason I'd insisted on talking to the both of them sooner rather than later.

"Sarah, I don't know why you don't like roses. And Rachel, you haven't really explained that either. But the number, twenty, still mystifies me. It has to mean something, and Rachel, I have a feeling that you're the only one, other than your father, who knows what that meaning is."

Now the tears were no longer silent. She was sobbing. Sarah kissed her hair and murmured, "Rach, honey, it's okay. He can't hurt you now. No one can. It's time, sweetheart. You have to let go of it now. Tell him. Tell him all of it."

Rachel cried, out, "I can't!. I just…can't. It's…too dirty. No one will ever forgive…" She started sobbing uncontrollably again, and I sat there listening to her wail, trying to speak, sounding like a penitent speaking in tongues. I wondered what other secret she could have more terrible than her father's sexual violation of her. I felt ashamed of myself for sitting there and listening.

When she finally managed to calm herself, she angled her face up and looked into Sarah's eyes. "It killed him. I killed him, Rach."

"No. No, you didn't, honey. If anybody killed him, it was your father."

Rachel let out a long, weary breath, settled back down onto Sarah's chest for a moment, then struggled up into a sitting position and stared down at her fingers, locked in mortal combat with each other, and began to speak. "The roses do mean something. The first time my father came to my bedroom, I was nine years old. The next morning there was a single red rose on my pillow. The following week, he visited me again in the middle of the night. The next morning, there were two roses nestled beside me. That night, while he was…touching me, I started crying and I couldn't stop. Finally, he left me. So after the second time, it was months before he returned. Not until after my tenth birthday…"

She sat there talking in a flat monotone voice, distanced from her words, staring over my shoulder. I could feel my heart thumping against my chest, a queasy feeling in the pit of my stomach.

"…he returned and left me that third rose. For the next three years, until he left us, he continued to add a rose to mark each… act. The last time, when I was thirteen, I found nineteen roses laying on the bed beside me. I hated them. They made me sick, just like he did. Each time, I'd get up, full of shame and guilt, sneak out of the house, and throw them in the woods behind our backyard so no one else would ever see them. To this day, I can't imagine why he did that. It seemed as bad as him touching me, entering me. It still does.

"When Sarah told me she got those twenty roses, I almost collapsed on the spot. I couldn't believe it. I didn't know what it meant. I assumed they came from my father, but I didn't know why. Why now? I hadn't told Sarah about the roses yet. I knew of her dislike for them. It was funny. It made me think we were somehow meant for each other. Silly, eh? But her disdain was normal, or, not really normal, she didn't like the look or smell. She didn't like association with love and Valentine's day, the phony marketing around it. She hated that little jeweler's ad, every kiss begins with K." She paused, couldn't help a grim half-smile and glance at Sarah, who forced a smile back at her.

She paused, squeezed her eyes tightly closed, her hands rolled into fists. Suddenly, she screamed, a howl of pent-up anger and revulsion.

"Oh Rachel," Sarah cried.

My blood ran cold.

The silence afterward was almost too much to bear.

A nurse appeared in the doorway, looking from the women to me and back again, her eyes wide with concern. "It's okay," I said. Sarah nodded, and the nurse left us.

Rachel opened her eyes, her face a mask of anguish, "I got a perfect, beautiful rose every time. And every time I got one more. Like each act, each violation, was to be celebrated. What did he want, Max? What did it mean to him? What was I supposed to do?"

I could hardly stand holding her gaze.

Her eyes stopped pinning me, slipped away. She shook her head, looking drained now, empty, lost, abandoned.

Sarah took her hand again and said, "Go ahead, Rach. Tell him the rest. He needs to know everything. If we're going to get the rat bastard, Mr. Plank needs to know the whole truth. He won't tell. I know he won't."

I was glad to have her trust, and I sure hoped that whatever Rachel told me was something that I could keep to myself.

Rachel tightened her grip on her friend's hand and said, "Okay…okay." For a moment, it looked like she was going to break down into tears again, but she gritted her teeth, let out a short grunt of determination. "Okay. Okay…

"That's all we had was each other. Mom stayed out of the house as much as she could manage. She must have felt so helpless. She adored him. God knows why. She didn't want to lose him. You'd never know it from the way she is now, but she was a meek lamb around him. I don't know if she ever tried to protect us. We were too young when it started, and by the time I was aware of her role, her responsibility, the fact that she should have done something…anyway, she never even acknowledged what went on in that house. To this day, she hasn't. None of us has."

Rachel closed her eyes, gathered herself, continued. "So Christopher and I had each other. We were all alone in the world. No one else could know. Could understand what we were going through. We became very close. We were best friends, spent all our time together when we were kids. I loved him. I loved him so much. We were everything to each other. Without him, I wouldn't have survived. Do you understand? Our connection was way beyond just brother and sister. We were survivors of the same war. Battle-hardened together is how he put it to me once not too long ago."

She looked into my eyes. A cold feeling, a tremor ran through me. I knew where this was going, and I didn't want to hear any more.

"I was sixteen the first time it happened. He was fourteen. I can't tell you how natural it felt. We knew it was wrong. We were petrified. But there was no way to avoid it. Until now, I've never had the same feeling," she stopped, winced. "Oh, no...sorry Sarah, I didn't mean to—"

"S-okay. I understand."

"Christopher was the only one who understood me. I'd found my soul mate, the boy I grew up with and suffered with. He felt the same way."

I felt like the breath had been knocked out of me.

"I know what you must think. Please, please don't tell anyone. I know how perverse it sounds. How awful and unforgivable."

I closed my eyes for a moment, and when I opened them, she was looking at me with a raw, unguarded look of such complete pain and, oddly, innocence, that I glimpsed the young girl inside her that had been fouled, despoiled by her own father, the same girl though, who hadn't been totally ruined, who'd survived by finding the only way out. Violating society's norms but staying alive.

Her brother, ultimately, hadn't been so fortunate.

"How long did it go on for?" I asked, as gently as I could.

She looked away. "Until six months ago..." Her voice broke, a catch in her throat, a small swallowed cry. "I know. Unbelievable. I'd tried. For a couple of years before that. But every time I mentioned it, Christopher would fall apart. He said he needed me. He couldn't live without me. He threatened to kill himself, more times than I can bear to remember." She stopped, her fingers twisting, turning, writhing like earthworms in a deep muddy.

"Finally, I cut it off completely. We'd been living together, but I told him he had to leave. He did, but he kept coming back. I changed the locks, stopped answering the door. It killed me to hurt him that way. He threatened again to kill himself. But I knew that my life was over if I didn't break it off. I still thought it was over for me...until I met Sarah."

"Did anyone else know or suspect? Your mother or father?"

"My mother knew. She found us one day. A couple of years after we started. When I was eighteen. She came home unexpectedly. She didn't see us…" A sharp intake of breath, her hands untangled and gripped her thighs. "But… Christopher was half-dressed, pulling on his pants. Our faces were flushed. I'll never forget the look on her face. The shock. For once, the mask she always wore slipped, and it was horrible to see. I just sat there on the couch wishing I was dead. Christopher rushed out of the room. She didn't say a word. After a while, she left me there alone. She never mentioned it again."

I couldn't imagine what it must have been like living in that house holding secrets big enough to destroy any adult's heart and soul, let alone a child's fragile ones.

"And your father didn't know because he wasn't there."

She nodded, then looked at me sharply. "He wasn't there because when he was thirteen, Christopher ran away and somehow ended up at the Children's Network—"

"What?" To say I was gobsmacked would be an understatement.

"I'm sorry. I should have told you. But, of all the terrible secrets that my family has, that one may be the most consequential. If it gets out, the family reputation will be ruined. Mother will be devastated."

I sat there rethinking everything I'd learned, questioning every revealed fact and clue that had brought me here. Perhaps they were all red herrings.

Staring at her hands, speaking in that flat, unaffected voice, she described how the Executive Director, Scott Tripp, was going to turn the evidence of Christopher's abuse over to the authorities before her mother intervened. She not only gave the Network the biggest donation they'd ever received, but promised to get her rich friends involved. She said Mr. Tripp played hard to get, acting as if this was an excruciating moral dilemma, but ultimately, he was swayed by the money and what he could do with it. Rachel also mentioned that as time went by, he seemed more and more entranced by his access to the creme de la creme of San Francisco society that Mrs. Wambaugh afforded.

Sarah broke in. "I guess it's time for me to come clean, too. I don't know if you know that I volunteered there for about a year. That's actually where I first met Christopher, although he didn't ask me out until he saw me perform at the club. He didn't volunteer there much, but I saw him once or twice."

Sarah paused, closed her eyes. "Sorry," she said. "Still feel pretty tired. I guess I'm not used to talking, eh?" She smiled weakly.

"I was there alone a few times. Once I was doing some work in Scott's office. He had me looking through a personnel file to get him some information, and I stumbled across a folder that'd he'd inadvertently left on his desk. It was Christopher's." She formed a pyramid with her hands, and her forefingers touched her lips. "It was all there. Just what Rachel said. The details of what Christopher had conveyed the night he'd run away and ended up there. I took photos of the files with my phone. There was nothing about the relationship between the Network and the Wambaughs or how his mother had paid Scott off. I didn't find that out until I asked Rachel about it and she filled in the details."

Rachel said, "Sarah wanted to expose it all. She tried to talk me into it. She was outraged. Thought the Children's Network, or at least Scott, had betrayed not only Christopher, but all the kids. She was right, of course. But I wasn't ready, I talked her into holding off, for the sake of my family, our business, my mother—"

"But I did confront Scott, and he had a fit. Said that I didn't know what I was talking about. That it was complicated and that he'd made sure Christopher was safe and protected. That his abuser was sent away. I quit working there. I kept at Rachel, and I agonized about just going ahead and talking to a reporter for the *Examiner.*"

"Did anyone else know about this. Your mother? Your father. Christopher?"

As I said it, I realized that Scott might very well have gone to Mrs. Wambaugh after his encounter with Sarah.

"Not that I know of," Rachel said.

But Sarah echoed my thought. "I'd guess Scott told her mom."

We sat there in silence for a while. I didn't know what they were thinking or trying not to think about. The implications of all this were pretty stark. A reason for murder? And who was the most likely culprit: Mrs. Wambaugh or her husband. Scott, although the wheelchair afforded him an alibi. Speed? Or the already fingered Christopher?

Rachel interrupted my thoughts. "What Scott told Sarah is right. He did extract a promise from mother that she would get my father away from us permanently. I guess he needed to salve his conscience somehow. Ever since, Mother has been the Children's Network's biggest benefactor. But her donations are anonymous, and her name is not even listed in the donor lists that they publish."

"So that's why your father left?"

"Yes. Scott was the one who finally freed us from him. But I sometimes think about what my father might be doing to other children, other innocents, and then I feel guilty as hell for keeping silent." She closed her eyes for a moment, then opened them and said, "No more. No more secrets. I don't care what happens to me or my mother or our damn company."

She shook her head, and her face crumbled again. She sobbed and choked the words out, "Even after he left, he was still there. His spirit dominated that awful house. We all tried to run away from him, but we never escaped. He haunted us every day. It caught up with Christopher. My mother…she…got swallowed up years ago. It's just me now and..." She closed her eyes, wrapped her arms around her body tight, collapsing into herself, her shoulders shaking like tree branches in a high wind. Sarah grabbed hold, cradling her, murmuring, almost singing to her, like a mother comforting her sick child.

THIRTY-FIVE

Q had the girl's cell phone number, but she wasn't taking calls. If she was anything like me, she had forgotten to charge her battery.

Q made some calls, narrowing down the possibilities until he got a reasonable lead and offered to take me to where he thought she might be holed up. He felt he should be there with me to make a formal introduction. It seemed like a good idea, especially considering the company he said she tended to keep.

He and Felicia were friends from way back, but it was hard now because of her increasing drug use and the kinds of people it had brought into her life. She'd been a beautiful girl. An innocent that got mixed up and messed up by Speed Weed, among others.

Q knew his way around addicts and hustlers. He was one of them, more or less. In another lifetime, he added, when his statement left me without a response.

As we were driving on over to see Felicia, Q got a call from Phoebe.

"Settle down, Phoeb. Take a breath. Gonna be okay."

He waited a few seconds and said, "You okay? Good. Talk to Q."

I could hear the sound of her, high-pitched, excited, sad, but couldn't make out many of the words. "Uh-Uh. Uh-uh. Right. Right. Okay. Sure. Good. Good. He doesn't deserve you, Phoebe. He gives you any more trouble, let me know, and I'll sick Henry on 'im. Or, better yet, our friend, Max. Here, talk to 'im."

I took the phone with my right hand, steadied the wheel with my left.

"Max, I don't wanna bother you."

"I'm bothered. That boyfriend of yours been acting up?"

She explained how they had a big fight over her not spending enough time in the kitchen catering to his needs. How he forbid her from going to see Sarah. How she told him to go to hell. How he slapped her. How she slapped him back. How he stormed out of the house. How she had the locks changed. How she was through with him.

"Good for you. But when he comes back, do you think a locked door is going to stop him?"

"I have a can of Mace."

"Right in the eyes," I said.

"Right in the eyes," she repeated solemnly.

"Or hit him over the head with one of your drumsticks. I've seen you play. You'll knock him out cold."

She laughed. I thought she'd be okay. I didn't get the impression that her boyfriend was dangerous, just a run-of-the-mill asshole. But I made sure she had my number and told her to call me if he came back and bothered her in any way.

THE MOTEL STAX, JUST OFF 16TH AVENUE AND GEARY, HAD SEEN better days. I didn't know if, back in its heyday, the owner had been a fan of Memphis soul—Booker T & his MG's, Otis Redding, the amazing Sam & Dave, the foot stomping rhythms of their great classic *Soul Man*, popped inside my head—and named his bright new enterprise after the famous record company, Motown's poor cousin.

Or maybe it was just a nonsense word. Maybe he liked flapjacks.

All this came into my mind via the inappropriate brain glitches I tend to have on a regular basis, sitting behind Q in his old Pontiac Coupe Deville, looking at the worn Stax Motel sign, the "a," "o," and "e" blurred with age.

Beneath the name, ownership touted vibrating beds, free television, brew your own coffee, and candy machines.

All that for sixty-nine bucks and change. I was surprised to see the vacancy sign.

I stood behind Q as he inquired of the desk clerk. The high-school-aged youth with more acne than facial hair wore a name tag that read *Welcome* on top, and *George* beneath it. He had an admirable sense of his fiduciary responsibility, apologetically refusing to divulge the name of any of the motel's guests.

I guessed the employee training regimen must have been intense, perhaps lasting the better part of a morning.

"George," I said. I glanced at his badge. "Welcome."

He angled his neck quizzically, like a puppy trying to determine if its owner had a treat in exchange for the trick he was demanding.

"Sir," he said, politely, immediately separating him from a young canine.

"I understand and appreciate motel policy. But, please, we need your help here. This is a touch and go situation. I can't say more. But I don't want to get the police involved. I don't want them coming here tonight. I think we can handle this quietly, keep from disturbing the other guests, if you'll just tell us what room Felicia is in. She'll be happy to see us, I can assure you of that."

As I spoke, his face morphed from an expression that indicated he was smelling a hint of poo poo to a more studied look resulting in a lower lip pout.

I smiled innocently, sincerely, imploringly.

"I don't know. If something happens, Del is going to blame me."

"Nothing's going to happen, except that you're going to have a very happy guest in room...?" I raised my eyebrows, opened my mouth slightly, anticipating.

"Twelve," he said, without thinking.

"In room twelve. Right. The police won't have to come bothering you. Poor Del won't ever know. I'm sure he's got enough problems, right?"

George nodded.

We left him there, before that smelling poo poo expression returned to his face.

FELICIA ANSWERED THE DOOR IN SOME KIND OF STATE.

She danced from one foot to the other, as if there were hot coals beneath her feet. "Oops," she said. "Say ho, Q."

"Ho," Q said, cooperatively. "Can we come in, Felicia?"

She nodded her head up and down, still rocking back and forth. "Sure can. You surely can."

Suddenly she grabbed him, hugged him tight to her body. She closed her eyes and mumbled, "Q, so nice to see you, Q," she said, repeating his name with a funny cadence.

With an awkward stumble, she stepped away and threw me a glance.

"That's Max. A friend."

She dipped her chin, turned, and went back inside.

Q followed her, and I followed him, closing the door behind me.

FELICIA SAT ON THE EDGE OF THE BED, HER RIGHT FOOT TAPPING out a rapid rhythm on the floor. Her hands played her thighs like drums, she was humming something that sounded like the Wicked Witch's marching castle guards in the Wizard of Oz's chanting: "O-EE-Yah! Eoh-Ah."

Her eyes were split wide, pupils were dilated, red-rimmed.

She sat up ram-rod straight, bristling with electricity, like she had a cattle-prod stuck up her spine.

Q pulled one of two joint-fractured particle board chairs up close to her.

I stood near the TV set nailed to high on the front wall of the unit.

"What you on, Felicia?"

She stopped humming her Oz-like chants and said, "Me?"

Q waited.

"Damn, Q. You know me. I'm high on life."

"Sure you are. I know that, girl. What's helpin' you love life so much right now?"

She laughed, jumped to her feet, danced to the side of the bed, picked up a pack of Camel Lights and a black lighter with the outline of a high-tailed cat on it. She lit up, inhaled, blew it out through her nose.

Held the cigarette out to Q. "Want one?"

"Not now, girl. Tell me."

"Damn. I miss you. I miss goin' out to the clubs with you. You knew everybody back then. And the way you taught me about music. God, I loved that. Way you treated me."

Q closed his eyes, sighed, rubbed the days-old growth of beard on his cheek.

"Yeah, Felicia. I miss those times, too."

He fixed her with a steady gaze, and she held it for a few

seconds, then her mouth drooped and she looked away. "You know how it is. I just do a little here and there…keep the blues away."

"I know, girl. The cops been talkin' to you any more about Speed?"

She took a long drag of the cigarette, then put it out on a blackened tray on the little bedside table. "Damn things," she said.

She came back to the bed, sat down, and said, "No I just had to go down to the police station the night he…passed. I told you all this. On the phone."

"Right, you did. But they ain't bothered you no more since?"

Her feet started up again, the floor catching fire.

"Felicia?"

"Uh-uh."

"And you just told 'em that you found him like that. Dead. You were just going to breakfast with him. You called 911 right away. You didn't know anything about the drugs he used or who gave them to him. That right?"

Felicia hunched over the bed, her fingers fiddling with the sheets, watching her dancing feet for a few beats before she mumbled, "Guess that's about it."

"And they didn't give you a hard time? Accuse you of anything?"

"One of them did. A little. Doing his job. But they was satisfied. They saw I was innocent."

"And were you?"

She looked up, the wrinkle lines around her eyes lengthening, her cheekbones sharp against the brittle bones beneath them. "What you sayin' to me right now, Q?"

"Nuthin'. Just askin'."

"Did you ever help Speed get drugs, Felicia?" I asked.

She frowned at me.

"He's okay. Don't worry. No matter what you tell him, just like me, we ain't gonna repeat it. He's the one helping find out who tried to kill Sarah Swan."

The expression on her face changed, softened, her lips curled into a half-smile. "Jesus, that girl can sing. I ain't seen her in 'most a year. When I heard what happened to her, I was so sorry feeling. Who could try to silence one of God's own angels?"

"That's right. That's why we're here. We're trying to find out who tried to kill Sarah. And maybe Speed too. We need to know everything you do. The truth. I know you didn't harm Speed. Whatever you can tell us stays here. No one else will ever know nuthin' unless you tell 'im."

She jumped to her feet, went over to a plastic coffee maker next to a little smoke-colored stand holding Folger's packets, creamer and sugar, and red swizzle sticks. She flipped the switch on the back of the machine, tore the brown crinkly Folger's paper open, flipped the lid and carefully lodged the packet of grounds inside, tapping it closed. She stood examining her work for a moment, before returning to the bed.

The machine buzzed, then commenced to snap, crackle, and pop.

Felicia's wrapped her arms around her shoulders, leaned way over her lap, as if she were trying to ward off blows.

"You saw him earlier, didn't you? Either the night before or early that morning. You brought him some stuff. You were just doing his bidding, right? He had a hold on you. I know that." Q spoke to her in a soft, empathic tone of voice.

She stayed rolled up tight, rocking back and forth on the bed, her voice strangled in her throat. "I didn't do what he said. Yeah, I took the money, but I didn't do it..."

"Who?" I said.

"I don't know his name..." she stopped, kept rocking silently.

With a final crack, the coffee machine wheezed and settled. I rose and poured the brew, half-filling two Styrofoam cups. "Cream, sugar?" I said.

Nobody answered, so I left one black for Q and put a little cream and sugar in the other. I went to the bed and tapped Felicia's shoulder. She lifted her head; there were tears in her eyes. She took the coffee, stayed hunched, but cradled the cup between her hands, steam rising up toward her nose. I offered the other cup to Q, who shook his head.

I took a sip, winced, sat down on the floor next to Q.

Felicia sipped on the coffee silently.

"What did he look like?" I asked.

She brushed her nose with the back of her hand, spilling a little coffee. "Damn!" She rubbed the wet, hot spots with her fingers, muttering to me at the same time, "Big. Crew cut white boy. Tan. No. Red like a beet. Not from around here."

Waldo, I thought, without having to think.

"What did he want?"

She downed the rest of the coffee in a gulp, dropped the Styrofoam to the floor. "Said he was a friend of an old friend of Speed's. Said he had something for him, something that Speed deserved. Said they thought I was the one who could benefit most from delivering it to him. Said they knew how bad Speed treated me. How he hit me. How he...oh, Q, how I'd ever end up in this place?"

She rolled up in a ball again, her body shaking to silent tears. Q touched her knee. "You just done the best you knew how. Made mistakes like all of us. Now it's time to make some changes. Make amends."

She eventually came out of it, wiped her eyes. Q went to the bureau and got her a box of Kleenex. She blew her nose, kept the tissue inside her clasped hand.

"What did this man give you for Speed?" I asked.

"A packet. He said it was cocaine like nuthin' else. Specially meant for Speed. Then he gave me an envelope, said it was for my trouble. He told me what to tell the police, said that they wouldn't bother me much. Speed was an addict. Nobody would care. But I'd be free. And I could get myself back on my feet with the five thousand dollars in that envelope."

"Lately, Speed been getting worse. He started loaning you out to his friends, Felicia, didn't he? When he was strung out bad. Desperate," Q asked. It was a question, but I thought he already knew the answer.

She kept her head down, but after a few moments, nodded affirmatively.

"He was a sick man. Nobody could blame you." Q's voice was grave, understanding, like a priest absolving a penitent of her sins.

Suddenly, she raised her head, her eyes shining. "I didn't. I couldn't. I took the money. After he left, I flushed the packet down the toilet. I'm ashamed of a lot of the things I've done. But my momma didn't raise no murderer. Speed wasn't a bad man. He was weak. But he done good things for me, too. Not just…those things he did when he was desperate…"

Some people were always looking for a silver lining. For the best in a person, no matter how awful their actions. These were the folk who defended guilty death row inmates and child molesters. I admired them, thought they were Christians after Jesus's own heart. But sometimes this open-hearted way of seeing and acting was self-defeating and ended in tragedy like what we had right here.

"Did you tell Speed about this man?" I asked.

"Yeah, the night before he died. He went wild. He was already high. I wanted to wait, but lately he was almost never sober. I was afraid. I'd kept the money. I didn't even know how to find the man who gave it to me. Speed told me it belonged to him. He told me to bring it to him. That's what I was doing the next morning when I found him. I didn't know what to think. I know he was pacing around like crazy before I left. He was trying to calm himself. Shouting about how they were coming to kill him. He'd snorted some coke, but he got his needle out...I told him not to. But he said he just needed to get calm so he could think. I shouldna' told him..."

She paused, shook her head sadly, then started up, as if she was doing an impromptu eulogy, recounting Speed's admirable qualities—his tenderness, how funny he could be, his love for music and women.

We just sat there listening. I didn't want to add to her grief and pain.

So I didn't tell her that tender, funny Speed had been the one who shot God's own angel, Sarah Swan.

THIRTY-SIX

I was back where it all began.

Outside the Black Canary, looking up at the sign advertising tonight's performer, Levon Smart, the bass guitarist for a semi-famous rock and blues band.

Levon was trying to strike out on his own. There'd been two cancelled tours by the semi-famous band in the past year and rumors of drug abuse, artistic differences, petty power squabbles.

Same old same old.

Levon's first solo album had hit iTunes last week. Tonight's show was the first in a long national tour of small clubs.

"Good luck," I said to the big black letters of his name. The sign was neon and would look a whole lot better tonight when it was dark.

It was mid-afternoon, the morning fog had lifted, and it was a beautiful but cold fall day. Winter, such as it is in San Francisco, was in the air.

I moved into the alleyway beside the Black Canary where I had chased Sarah's shooter and made my way back to the Children's Network.

I'D CONFIRMED THAT SCOTT TRIPP WAS THERE BUT NEGLECTED TO inform him that I was on my way.

The front door wasn't locked. I gathered that they only secured the offices at night.

I stepped inside, and a young woman with a bright smile welcomed me. She told me her name was Tiffany, and I told her I was Max and here to see Scott, that he was expecting me, and that I would find my own way to his offices, affecting overfamiliarity to disarm her.

As I stepped around her, her brow furled up into a look of puzzled consternation, but I guessed, young as she was, that she still trusted in the general beneficence of mankind.

I reached the back of the offices, located Scott's likely domain, glanced in the doorway, confirming he was hard at work hunched over this desk examining spreadsheets. I stepped in, reached back, and shut the door behind me, noticing Tiffany, who had followed me tentatively, and was examining me with a searching but hopeful look.

I gave her a big smile and closed the door.

By the time I turned, Scott had looked up from his desk. I didn't take his unfriendly frown personally.

I grabbed a teak chair with a plush white cushion and spun it so the back faced me. I sat down and placed my arms on top of the backrest.

Scott dispensed with the polite formalities. "What do you want?"

"Hello, Scott. I want to talk to you about your and the Children's Network's relationship with Mrs. Wambaugh and Wambaugh Enterprises."

"You'll have to make an appointment. I'm busy right now. Although, I have no intention of talking to you about our relationship with any of our benefactors. Now," he stretched, yawned, flexed his hands backward, then put them down firmly on the armrests of his wheelchair, "if you'll please let yourself out the same way you came, I'll—"

"When you started this up, I bet you never imagined you'd be protecting child abusers."

He just looked at me.

"You let yourself be used. For money. For attention from society's upper crust."

His eyes narrowed, his face tightened, his fingers reddened from the intensity of his grip on the wheelchair.

"That was the beginning of it. You couldn't resist. Not when Mrs. Wambaugh came to you and pleaded to keep what you knew about Christopher private and away from the media. Not when she offered you all that money and all that access to her friends."

"That's not—"

"You didn't know then that it would eventually lead to you being an accomplice in an attempted murder. But that's how it works sometimes, one misstep, one betrayal of our principles, puts us on a—"

"I had nothing to do with the shooting," he sputtered. "I didn't—"

"You're going to resign your position here today. And you're going to get Liz to resign too, because, for whatever reason, she protected Speed Weed, and you." I figured Liz and Scott were romantically entangled.

"You're out of your mind," he growled, his face scrunched up, his eyes shooting daggers of contempt.

"Sarah Swan is ready to go public with what she saw in Christopher's file. And Rachel Wambaugh will back her up with information about the payoff from her family to you. I don't know if you pocketed any of the money personally, but either way, it's dirty money, earned by betraying your mission to protect abused children. The papers, and the local television reporters, will have a field day with you. Your funding and support in the community will vanish."

The contempt dropped from his face, replaced by a sudden startled look, like a streetwalker caught in a patrol car's spotlight.

"I don't know how much you knew about the attempt on Sarah's life. But I know that Speed Weed escaped through your offices. And that you covered for him. If I tell the police about that, and I should, you'll be an accomplice to murder, a felony conviction just around the corner. I'm letting you off the hook easy. But my offer is only good for one day. Hand in your and Liz's resignations to the board by the end of the day today, or it'll be the ruin of the Network."

I knew that this was his life's work. That he lived for the Network. That losing it would be like losing a child to him.

And I didn't really want Sarah and Rachel to have to go suffer going through the media hoopla surrounding any kind of scandal of this sort. As far as Scott's involvement with Sarah's shooting, I had no firm evidence. But I knew both he and Liz had been complicit.

Without saying another word, I left him there, hanging his head, his hands limp on the armrests, his eyes downcast.

He was a beaten man, but I didn't feel even a tinge of sympathy for him. Not after all I'd heard and seen from Rachel and Sarah. Not after poor Christopher's death.

THIRTY-SEVEN

Mrs. Wambaugh stepped onto my boat for the second, and last, time in the waning dusk of a biting cold September day.

There was no driver this time; she'd piloted the Cadillac limousine parked out on the dock herself.

She wasn't happy to be here on my boat, my floating home.

I'd insisted though. Told her that I had important news. Told her that I had news about Rachel and that if she didn't want a big surprise on the evening news, she'd best get on over to my humble floating home ASAP.

A long silence followed my urging and then she said simply, "Six p.m.," and hung up.

I had the side door to the cabin open, and she ducked and entered, her eyes quickly taking in the surroundings, confirming things hadn't changed for the better.

I sat at a hardwood swiveling captain's chair. She glanced at me, frowned, looked around. I pointed to the small fraying leather couch opposite me, on the starboard side of the boat.

I neglected to offer her a greeting or any refreshments.

I didn't want to waste her time or mine. I already knew the answers to most of the questions I was going to ask her and figured she wouldn't tell me the truth anyway. I was just hoping she might clear up a couple of the less consequential, but still important, details that were driving me crazy.

"All right. You have me here. Tell me what was so important. I hope you're not just wasting my time again."

She wore an ankle-length snow-leopard-colored fur coat, opened at the neck with tight, tailored black pants and classic high-heeled shoes. A small leather handbag was looped around her left wrist. Her hair was pulled back and away from her fore-head, secured with a golden metal clasp. Her makeup was thick, as usual, applied painstakingly. Her facial features were compressed, shrunken, her lips pulled back and drawn as was her pallor.

I picked up a manila folder on my lap, opened it, glanced through my notes.

"I despise you. You are responsible for my son's death. I'm still talking to my lawyers and, despite their misgivings, I intend to press charges for breaking and entering and whatever else is remotely possible."

I raised my eyes from the folder and looked directly into hers. "I just don't get the roses, Mrs. W. That, to me, is almost worse than hiring somebody to kill Sarah."

Her eyes continued to hold mine, but her cheeks flinched. Her hands began to tremble. Her fingers clutched at the purse. She stood up.

"Sit down," I barked.

She obeyed.

"I'm not expecting any response from you. But you're going to listen to me. Do you understand?"

Her eyes flared, her face reddened, and she snarled, "I don't have to listen to a God damn—"

"I know everything. *Everything.* Rachel told me. I believe you'll want to hear me out and find out what's going to happen next."

She exhaled loudly, but the fight went out of her a little. She rubbed her hands together, seeking warmth, solace. She wasn't going to get it from me.

"So just listen. That's all you have to do."

She glanced back at me, then away again. A proud woman bending, reluctantly, but still bridling at the humiliation of having to sit and listen to a man of my class and bearing.

"You hired Speed Weed to kill Sarah Swan." I lifted a small torn piece of note paper that I'd taken from Speed's house. "He mentions you here: Mrs. W. He also notes several dates. One the Thursday before Sarah was shot. It says G. Pick Up. Another two days after when he met you at the bridge at Lake Merced in Daly City. It says G. Drop off. I assume that means gun. Then a dollar sign. I assume these were written before the meetings, not after. A couple of other dates are mentioned, weeks before the shooting. Meetings scheduled with Mrs. W. To work out the plan, the details. What he'd get paid. I imagine you got off cheap, considering his anger, his pent-up hated toward Sarah."

"You're despicable."

"We've already established that. Believe me, I've come to my peace about it. I'm sure you took Christopher's gun because Speed didn't want to buy one. I'm sure you weren't trying to implicate him in the crime. You wanted to get rid of the gun after he gave it back to you, but you didn't. You meant to. I don't know where you hid it, but Christopher found it. That was more than thoughtless, Mrs. Wambaugh. Perhaps you didn't think there was a chance he'd try to commit suicide again. But I'd say you were criminally negligent. 'Course that wasn't exactly the first time you were that toward both of your children."

She stood up again. If looks could kill, yours truly would be ashes in an urn right now. But I glared right back at her. I had to give her credit. She stayed strong. She didn't break down under my assault. She did sit herself back onto the sofa.

"But I guess that's not important now. Your husband had ruined Christopher. And you'd done nothing to stop it. You stood by while he abused your son and violated your daughter. And you used the roses, the instruments by which he further humiliated her, rubbed her nose in it, to somehow send a signal to the woman she loved before your hired hand shot her."

She sat there like a stone-cold statue, giving me nothing.

"By sending twenty roses to Sarah, you reveal that you knew what each of the nineteen previous deliveries meant. You are complicit in your daughter's sexual assault. You are guilty of so much more than attempted murder. You are beneath—"

"Stop," she shouted. Her hands gripped the couch, grasping for purchase. "My husband was a flawed individual. He had weaknesses. I won't deny it. But Rachel was not the innocent that she claims to be. She was precocious. She used her charms with her father, always getting what she wanted. I don't know what went on between them. Not really. And yes, he had a temper. He sometimes was too harsh with Christopher..." a hitch in her voice, but she caught it, steeled herself, continued, "with me. That's why I sent him away. I did act."

"She was nine years old for crissakes. Nine!"

She sighed and shook her head dismissively as if I didn't understand the wily ways of nine-year-old girls.

I thought I'd heard just about every kind of rationalization of the worst kinds of crimes. But this took self-justification to a whole new level.

"But that doesn't mean I stopped loving my husband. I visited him. Every few weeks, we met. Here and there. He loved me, in his own way. But I couldn't let our family business, the business my father built, sacrificing so much, time with his family, his health. I wouldn't let our name be besmirched with the tawdry, the vile secrets of a weak man and my children. I certainly wasn't going to let any low-class shrew ruin our reputation, built over generations. Ms. Swan stuck her nose where it didn't belong..." She stopped herself, studying me, perhaps wondering if I was wearing a wire.

"You have to be kidding me," I said.

"Make light of it. Someone like you has no sense of pride in something greater than yourself. An institution, a business worth preserving. A respected family name. I wasn't going to let it, us, be drawn through the mud. The jokes and disparagements of shallow people like you."

I was astonished. I don't what I expected from her that day, but what I got was much worse than anything I'd imagined. I sat there trying to absorb all this new information, and suddenly, I had a flash of understanding.

"Speed never met your husband. He never talked to him directly, did he?"

She just looked at me.

"You said you continued to meet with your husband. Talk with him. You never told Rachel and Christopher. Maybe you felt you were protecting them or maybe you were afraid they'd wouldn't understand the depth of your betrayal as their mother." I paused, still thinking, putting together my theory as I talked. "So Speed kept contacting you. Maybe you were smart enough not to give him your unlisted number. Maybe he showed up unexpectedly at your house. He wanted more money. He realized you'd gotten off cheap. You were angry because he'd failed to kill Sarah. Both of you were pissed off, but you realized that he was a risk. His drug use was getting worse, his state of mind deteriorating. You didn't know what he'd say to whom. So you told your husband who sent Waldo to see Felicia. Is that about right?"

She didn't give me a thing.

Stone. Cold. Statue.

"Maybe you don't even know, but you didn't kill Speed. He overdosed all by himself. Although Waldo may have hastened the end with his lame attempt."

She looked like she wanted to ask a question but remained silent. I wasn't going to tell her anymore anyway. I believed that what I had just recounted was as close to the truth as I was going to get. It made sense and explained William's outburst in the Chairman's suite.

Suddenly, she blurted out, "I didn't send roses to Sarah. It was Christopher. Trying to get back at his sister for abandoning him."

I didn't know whether she was telling the truth, but guessed she was. Why would she bother to deny it? Why would this stick in her craw, among all the other despicable acts she'd committed? Christopher had been desperate, falling apart, he may have lashed out in desperation, trying to impress on Rachel what she'd done to him by hooking up with Sarah.

In any event, I was tired of it. Tired of her. I wanted her gone. I never wanted to see her again. I was worried about Frankie and Alexandra and Fogerty's threats. But even as we spoke here, I knew he was about to be neutralized.

"I can't listen to you anymore, Mrs. W. But I have just one more question. Why did you hire me in the first place?" I thought I knew the answer but wanted to hear it from the snake's tongue.

She looked at me. She shook her head. She sighed. She closed her eyes and mumbled, "The worst decision I ever made..." Her voice trailed off in what sounded to me like despair.

Made my day.

"It was your alibi, right? Why would you try and murder the person that you hired an investigator to investigate? Your try at a sleight of hand, a shell game. Look here, not there."

She remained silent.

I shrugged.

She changed topics. "What are you going to do with your silly notes there? Your ridiculous evidence? Are you going to tell your fantasy tale to the police? To Detective Marley. Go right ahead. There isn't a shred of credible—"

"What do you think led me to connect you and Speed?" I said.

Her body went rigid, her face drained of color. She hadn't forgotten that I was in her bedroom; she was still threatening to sue me for trespassing. "I have photos of your handwriting confirming meetings with S.W. on dates corresponding to his notes. I have a receipt for a purchase of the gun. I thought Christopher purchased it, but it was in your files. Your bank statement on the day after the shooting, shows a withdrawal from Bank of America of fifteen-thousand dollars in cash. That's how much you paid Speed. Not a lot of money for you, but cash. I'd like to trace that money. Perhaps you could come up with credible purchases to account for all or most of it, perhaps not. What I have may not be enough to convict you in a court of law. I don't even know if Sarah would want that. But I'll bring this all to her. I'll tell her and Rachel all about our conversation, starting with your belief that she seduced her own father."

She was as white as bedsheets pulled out of a hot dryer. "She won't believe you," she sputtered.

"Your daughter isn't stupid. And she lived with you for almost twenty years. She'll believe me. Now get off my boat."

Her mouth opened, then snapped shut. She got to her feet, trembling with some combination of anger or indignation or worry. I doubted there was much guilt.

As she passed through my front door and stepped onto the dock, I said, "If I were you, I wouldn't want to miss the nightly news tonight."

THIRTY-EIGHT

We were all sitting in the lounge of the *Sweet and Sour* waiting on the ten p.m. news.

Meiying and Frankie were hunched over a card table munching on microwave popcorn and playing Crazy Eights.

I was at the bar in the middle of a cribbage thrashing from Dao, feeling happy to be losing. Things were back to normal.

Fabrice had called the previous night and asked if I had time to speak with her boss, George Liu.

When George got on the phone, he launched right into the fact that he'd had a long talk with his nephew, Takeshi. He said his nephew had disputed some of my facts, but basically admitted to "overzealous actions."

That was one way to put it. Overzealous to the max.

He paused, and I heard some shuffling around on the other end of the line. He muttered something to Fabrice, then came back onto the line. "Takeshi gave his apologies. He spoke in the manner I expected. Telling me the words I wanted to hear."

"So where does that leave us? Can you promise that he won't—"

"Wait. Listen. Takeshi now lives in Chengdu. In China. With my family. Despite the fact that he said the words that needed to be said, there was no force behind them. No truth."

"I see. So, he agreed to go to China?"

Liu chuckled. "He found that his choices were limited. He is going to school there. He has a guardian. He will not return to America for a long time."

"Thank you, Mr. Liu. That will be a relief to Dao and Meiying."

"Offer them my sincerest apologies, please. I will send them a letter soon along with a sincere gift."

Meiying hugged me tight when I told her the news, and Dao expressed his appreciation sincerely by showing no mercy at cribbage.

On the sixty-inch big screen television attached to the upper wall opposite the bar, an excited female voice trumpeted the headlines to come. The second story was the one I'd been waiting for. The multimillionaire husband of the owner of Wambaugh Enterprises, Mr. William Fogerty, being led out of the Palazzo Hotel in Las Vegas in handcuffs accused of sexually molesting his daughter.

Take that, Mrs. Wambaugh. How's that for dragging the family name through the mud?

Marsh, sitting next to Dao, was studying architectural plans for the Kabuki theater. He looked up at the TV and whistled. "I wonder what great-great granddad, that snake oil salesman, would think about all this?"

"Even that carnival barker might be ashamed. Far as I know, he didn't molest little girls."

Meiying said, "Max! Shush!"

I blushed. I wasn't used to having to watch my words around little girls.

"Don't worry, Meiying. I know all about bad men and little girls," Frankie insisted.

"No. No. Too young, Frankie," Meiying cried.

I felt the same way.

LATER, AFTER DAO AND MEIYING HAD GONE TO BED AND FRANKIE was asleep on the couch in the lounge, Marsh and I stepped outside to the back deck where I sipped decaf espresso and he did the same to a glass of Cognac.

I brought him up to date on the week of excitement he'd missed.

"You need me, buddy," he concluded.

"Never said I didn't. Doesn't stop you from disappearing every now and then."

"Duty calls."

I didn't bother asking him if the duty was to God, or mankind, or country. He never gave me any specifics. I had the feeling that he didn't want me to know something that might somehow endanger me. In any case, I'd learned staring down that rabbit hole was a waste of time.

"But I sure wish you and I could have paid William Fogerty a visit at the Palazzo."

"Yeah. Sounds like a good time."

"But I guess the way it turned out is even worse for him overall. He would have suffered physically if we'd surprised him, but this way, he'll likely end up behind bars for the rest of his days. Couldn't happen to a more deserving guy."

"You sure Rachel's willing to go all the way with it?"

"I think so. Sarah's behind her. And she feels absolutely no sympathy for the man. He's related to her by blood, but she sees him clearly as the twisted predator he is."

"And neither of them wants to go after Mrs. Wambaugh?"

"I hesitated telling Rachel the truth. I debated how much to

say, how much of my talk with that pathetic woman she could
bear. I started out skirting around the really nasty stuff. But I
could soon see she had few illusions left about her mother. So I
told her everything. She was most shocked, felt most betrayed, by
the fact that she'd maintained a husband-wife relationship all
these years while keeping them in the dark. That and the fact that
her mother actually blamed her for some of the sexual stuff,
essentially saying she preyed on his weaknesses. Imagine hearing
that from your own mother."

"I can't," Marsh said, staring out at the subdued lights of the
big boats surrounding us. "My mother thought I was the cat's
meow. The sun rose and set on my little brow."

"Another kind of delusion."

"Or clairvoyant. So, Rachel was able to handle it, after all?"

"Better than I expected. Having Sarah helps."

"But they're going to let the attempted murder slide?"

"I wouldn't put it that way. It would be hard to convict her.
The stuff I took from her house would be thrown out. The rest is
circumstantial. Speed's notes are too sketchy. She has a harem of
high-priced lawyers."

Speed Weed has pulled the trigger, attempting to kill Sarah.
But he wasn't the only, or even main culprit. Mrs. W. bore even
greater guilt, as did William Fogerty. Guilty as sin. Scott Tripp
was also culpable. All of them deserved to suffer for their deeds
and omissions, and I trusted, the way things were turning out,
that they would.

I reflected a little more on my reflections and then continued,
"And, with Rachel's testimony against her father pending, they
can't imagine being involved in another criminal case. Neither
one of them has the stomach for it. Mrs. Wambaugh is certainly
no longer a threat."

It all made sense, and I agreed with the women's decision. Mrs.

Wambaugh was all alone now. Her husband, her secret affair, was going to jail for the rest of his life. Her son was dead. Her daughter would never speak to her again.

She still had Manderley, but it seemed she was condemned to live there all alone now, in a prison of her own making.

THIRTY-NINE

"Uncle Max, you've never been married, have you?"

Jen, Bo Fiddler's lovely, sweet, daughter, married now for almost one year, knew that I'd never taken the plunge, but maybe she was just making sure I hadn't neglected to mention some ex-mail-order bride.

We were in the kitchen of her small rental house in Haight-Ashbury. I looked out the greenhouse window, dotted with little cacti, and watched Frankie doing amazing tricks on her skateboard.

"No, honey, never have."

"Well, it changes things. I know you have Alexandra. I don't know exactly how much time you spend together, whether you're in her bed a lot or a little, but even living together without being married isn't the same. Before…"

I let her speak. I didn't want to go into how much time I spent in Alexandra's bed, although lately it sure was feeling like not nearly enough.

"Brad is the same Brad I fell in love with. But he's changed too. He's more serious. Not as much fun. He doesn't like his job.

Doesn't know what he wants to do. Before, I was enough for him…"

As she continued, trying to explain the unfathomable mysteries of a relationship, of a loved one's mysteries, I almost regretted promising Bo I'd come and talk to her. But Bo, against his better judgment, had helped me out with the Wambaugh party, and I owed him. I tuned back into Jen's philosophical musings.

"…and so, we fight now. We didn't used to ever do that."

I love Jen. I've known her all my life. I was Uncle Max. But she'd broken my cardinal rule of never ever marrying before the age of thirty, and even that was risky. Forty was better. Forgetting the whole thing best. I sighed internally and put my cynicism aside.

"Sweetie, the two of you are still adjusting to your life together. The first year of marriage, from what I've heard, can be tough on some couples. Others don't feel it until the second year or the sixth. But the problems always come. You're lucky maybe that you have to deal with them right away. Maybe you can solve them early and it'll be smooth sailing for the next fifty years."

It was my voice speaking, but I didn't know who the hell was giving this Pollyanna advice.

"Do you really think so?"

"Sure," I lied.

"It's just that I can tell he's unhappy. Maybe it's me. Maybe he's disappointed. I try not to nag him. I wish he knew what he wanted to do, but I don't—"

"He's working for a contractor?"

"A termite inspector. But he doesn't like crawling under houses looking for bugs."

I couldn't blame the boy. "How about college?"

"It's not his thing."

The choices had to be more varied than bugs or college.

"What about you? I thought you were going to be a vet."

"Yeah. Maybe. Right now, we need the money I make."

She worked as a waitress at a diner in the Haight.

"Your dad will help."

"We want to stand on our own."

Admirable, but maybe not so smart.

"You've been going to therapy?" Another area where I had no direct experience.

"Yes. We started together, but it's just me now. Brad didn't like it. I do. It helps me."

"Good. Keep going then."

I hardly knew the man who was giving this sage advice. I'd sooner have my spleen removed than go to a therapist.

"Well," I said. "We have to get to the airport to pick up Alexandra. Will you promise to meet me for lunch sometime after the holidays? Check in with me. Let me know how things are going?"

So I could let Bo know that his daughter was doing okay.

"Sure, Uncle Max. I think you're right, Everything will be all right. Brad will figure it out, and I'll support him, and we're going to have an amazing fifty years ahead of us."

"Don't sell yourself short. Life spans are lengthening. I think you've got at least seventy years."

She beamed. I beamed back, feeling like a big, fat, phony, but a quite decent uncle.

FORTY

Frankie held my hand as we waited at baggage claim number four at San Francisco International Airport.

She kept on jumping up on her toes, trying to see if she could spot Alexandra.

"Do you see her, Max? Do you?"

"Not yet." I wasn't up on my tiptoes, but my insides were kind of jumping up and down, too. She'd been away for more than three weeks on an assignment that kept on being extended.

Five more minutes passed. It had been fifteen minutes since her flight landed.

Where was she?

"Where is she?"

"If she was in the back of the plane, it takes a long time to get off, hon."

"I'm going to tell her to sit near the front from now on."

"Good idea."

I spotted her just before the escalator deposited her on the first floor. I waved. "There she is."

"Where! Where?" Frankie shouted, jumping up the air.

I picked her up, waved to her, pointed. "Right there."

Frankie jumped to the floor and ran straight to Alexandra, who had a big beautiful smile on her face. She picked Frankie up and hugged her tight against her chest. She kept walking, murmuring in Frankie's ear while the little girl chattered.

Alexandra fixed me with a look that made my heart skip a couple of beats.

I watched the two of them there hugging, and I felt such a longing that something inside me threatened to break away, pull apart. Something from which I might not recover.

I didn't feel like myself. I was having thoughts that I didn't want to have.

Alexandra kept looking at me, stripping me bare.

C'mon Max, it's okay. You aren't breaking any rules.

You're older than forty.

AUTHOR NOTE

Hello Dear Reader,

You made it to the end of the book and I hope you enjoyed the journey.

Thanks for giving me your valuable time. I surely appreciate it.

What I would also greatly appreciate is if you could give other readers the benefit of your experience. Could you take a few moments to go to Amazon and leave an honest review?

Reviews are essential for others to discover my work and for me to keep telling stories.

Thank you!!!

ABOUT THE AUTHOR

Robert Bucchianeri is the author of the Max Plank Mystery Series along with the suspense thriller, Between a Smile and a Tear, the psychological thriller, Ransom Dreams, the rock n'roll mystery, Acapella Blues, as well as the sunlit noir, Love Stings. He is also the author of the novella, Jet: The Fortress, an espionage thriller. Along with his wife, son, and wonder dog, Buddy, he resides, mostly, on Cape Cod.

For More Information
https://rjbucchianeri.com